"THEY MURDERED OUR EARTH. IT'S ALL BLACK AND SMOKING. DEAD AS THE MOON!"

Donnan beat one fist against the bulkhead. It was coming home to him too, forcing its way past every barrier he could erect, the full understanding of what had been done. Maybe so far he'd been saved from shivering into pieces by the habit of years, tight situations, violence and death from New Mexico to New Guinea, Morocco to the Moon—and beyond— but habit was now crumpling in him too; presently he'd ram the pistol barrel up his mouth.

And then the siren blew again, and Strathey's voice filled the ship: "Battle stations! Prepare for combat! Three unidentified objects approaching, six o'clock low. They seem to be nuclear missiles. Stand by for evasive action and combat!"

POUL ANDERSON

AFTER DOOMSDAY

BAEN SCIENCE FICTION BOOKS

AFTER DOOMSDAY

Copyright © 1961, 1962 by Poul Anderson

A Baen Book

Baen Publishing Enterprises
260 Fifth Avenue
New York, N.Y. 10001

First Baen printing, September 1986

ISBN: 0-671-65591-4

Cover art by David Egge

Printed in the United States of America

Distributed by
SIMON & SCHUSTER
TRADE PUBLISHING GROUP
1230 Avenue of the Americas
New York, N.Y. 10020

I

For man also knoweth not his time: as the fishes that are taken in an evil net, and as the birds that are caught in the snare; so are the sons of men snared in an evil time, when it falleth suddenly upon them.

—Ecclesiastes, ix, 12

"EARTH IS DEAD. They murdered our Earth!"

Carl Donnan didn't answer at once. He remained standing by the viewport, his back to the others. Dimly he was aware of Goldspring's voice as it rose towards a scream, broke off, and turned into the hoarse belly-deep sobs of a man not used to tears. He heard Goldspring stumble across the deck before he said, flat and empty:

"Who are 'they'?"

But the footfalls had already gone out of the

1

door. Once or twice in the passageway beyond, Goldspring evidently hit a bulkhead, rebounded and lurched on. Eventually he would reach the stern, Donnan thought, and what then? Where then could he run to?

No one else made a sound. The ship hummed and whispered, air renewers, ventilators, thermostats, electric generators, weight-maintainers, the instruments that were her senses and the nuclear converter that was her heart. But the noise was no louder in Donnan's ears than his own pulse. Nor any more meaningful, now. The universe is mostly silence.

There was noise aplenty on Earth, he thought. Rumble and bellow as the crust shook, as mountains broke open and newborn volcanoes spat fire at the sky. Seethe and hiss as the oceans cooled back down from boiling. Shriek and skirl as winds went scouring across black stone continents which had lately run molten, as ash and smoke and acid rain flew beneath sulphurous clouds. Crack and boom as lightning split heaven and turned the night briefly vivid, so that every upthrust crag was etched against the horizon. But there was no one to hear. The cities were engulfed, the ships were sunk, the human race dissolved in lava.

And so were the trees, he thought, staring at that crescent which hung grey and black and visibly rolling against the stars; so were grass in summer and a shout of holly berries in snow, deer in the uplands of his boyhood, a whale he once saw splendidly broaching in a South Pacific dawn, and the bean-flower's boon, and the blackbird's tune, and May, and June. He turned back to the others.

Bowman, the executive officer, had laid himself on the deck, drawn up his knees and covered his face. Kunz the astronomer and Easterling the planetographer were still hunched over their instruments, as if they would find some misfunction that would give the lie to what they could see with unaided eyes. Captain Strathey had not yet looked away from the ruin of Earth. He stood with more-than-Annapolis straightness and the long handsome countenance was as drained of expression as it was of colour.

"Captain," Donnan made himself say. "Captain, sir—" He waited. The silence returned. Strathey had not moved.

"Judas in hell!" Donnan exploded. "Your eyeballs gone into orbit around that thing out there?" He made three strides across the bridge, clapped a hand on Strathey's shoulder and spun him around. "Cut that out!"

Strathey's gaze drifted back towards the viewscreen. Donnan slapped him, a pistol noise at which Kunz started and began to weep.

"Look here," Donnan said between his teeth, "men in the observatory satellites, in the Moon bases, in clear space, wouldn't'a been touched. We've got to raise them, Find out what happened and—and begin again, God damn us." His tone wobbled. He swore at himself for it. "Bowman! Get on the radio."

Strathey stirred. His lips went rigid, and he

said in almost his old manner, "I am still the master of this ship, Mr. Donnan."

"Good. I thought that'd fetch you." Donnan let him go and fumbled after pipe and tobacco. His hands began to shake so badly that he couldn't get the stuff out of his pockets.

"I—" Strathey squeezed his eyes shut and knuckled his forehead. "A radio signal might attract . . . whoever is responsible." The tall blue-jacketed body straightened again. "We may have to risk it later. But for the present we'll maintain strict radio silence. Mr. Kunz, kindly make a telescopic search for Earth satellites and have a look at the Moon. Mr. Bowman—*Bowman!*—prepare to move ship. Until we know better what's afoot, I don't want to stay in an obvious orbit." He blinked with sudden awareness. "You, Mr. Donnan. You're not supposed to be here."

"I was close by, fetching some stuff," the engineer explained. "I overheard you as you checked the date." He paused. "I'm afraid everybody knows by now. Best order the men to emergency stations. If I may make a suggestion, that is. And if you'll authorize me to take whatever measures may be needed to restore order, I'll see to that for you."

Strathey stared at him for a while. "Very good," he said, with a jerky sort of nod. "Carry on."

Donnan left the bridge. Something to do, he thought, someone to browbeat, anything so as to get over these shakes. Relax, son, he told himself. The game's not necessarily over.

Is it worth playing further, though?

By God, yes. As long as one man is alive and prepared to kick back, it is. He hurried down the passageway with the slightly rolling gait that remained to him of his years at sea: a stocky, square-shouldered man of medium height in his mid-thirties, sandy-haired, grey-eyed, his face broad and blunt and weathered. He wore the blue zipsuit chosen for comfort as well as practicality by most of the *Franklin's* crew, but a battered old R.A.F. beret slanted athwart his brow.

Other men appeared here and there in the corridor, and now he could hear the buzz of them, like an upset beehive, up and down the ship's length—three hundred men, three years gone, who had come back to find the Earth murdered.

Not just their own homes, or their cities, or the United States of America. *Earth*. Donnan checked himself from dwelling on the distinction. Too much else to do. He entered his cabin, loaded his gun and holstered it. The worn butt fitted his palm comfortably; he had found use for this Mauser in a lot of places. But today it was only a badge, of course. He could not shoot perhaps one three-hundredth of the human species. He opened a drawer, regarded the contents thoughtfully, and took out a little cylinder of iron. Clasped in his fist, it would add power to a blow, without giving too much. He dropped it in a pocket. In his days on the bum, when he worked for this or that cheap restaurant and expected trouble, the stunt had been to grab a roll of nickels.

He went out again. A man came past, one of the civilian scientists. His mouth gaped as he walked. Donnan stepped in front of him. "Where are you going, Wright?" he asked mildly. "Didn't you hear the hooter?"

"Earth," Wright cried from jaws stretched open. "The Earth's been destroyed. I saw. In a viewscreen. All black and smoking. Dead as the Moon!"

"Which does not change the fact that your emergency station is back that-a-way. Come on, now, march. We can talk this over later on."

"You don't understand! I had a wife and three children there. I've got to know— Let me by, you bastard!"

Donnan put him on the deck with a standard devil's handshake, helped him up, and dusted him off. "Be some use to what's left of the human race, Wright. It was your family's race too." The scientist moved away, quaking but headed in the proper direction.

A younger man had stopped to watch. He spat on the deck. "What human race?" he said. "Three hundred males?"

The siren cut loose again, insanely.

"Maybe not," Donnan answered. "We don't know yet. There were women in space as well as men. Get on with your job, son."

He made his way aft, arguing, cajoling, once or twice striking. Strathey told him over the intercom that the other decks were under control. Not that there had been much trouble. Most personnel had gone to their posts as directed . . . the way Donnan had seen cattle go down a stockyard chute. A working minority still put some snap into their movements. He might have been astonished, in some cases, at what people fitted which category—big Yule, for instance, who had saved three men's lives when the storm broke loose on Ubal, or whatever the heathenish name of that planet had been, now uselessly wailing, and mild little Murdoch the linguist locating someone else to man Yule's torpedo tube—but Donnan had knocked around too much in his day to be surprised at anything people did.

When he felt the quiver and heard the low roar as the U.S.S. *Benjamin Franklin* got under way, he hesitated. His own official post was with his instruments, at the No. 4 locker. But—

There was little sense of motion. The paragravitic drive maintained identical pseudo-weight inboard, whether the ship was in free fall or under ten gravities' acceleration . . . or riding the standing waves of space at superlight quasi-speed, for that matter. Everything seemed in order. Too much so, even. Donnan preferred more flexibility in a crew. With sudden decision, he turned on his heel and went down the nearest companionway.

Ramri of Monwaing's Katkinu rated a suite in officer country, though much of this was devoted to storage of the special foods which he required and which he preferred to cook for himself. Donnan tried the door. It opened. He stepped through, closed and latched it behind him, and said. "You bloody fool."

The being who sat in a spidery aluminum framework rose with habitual gracefulness. Puzzlement blurred, for a moment, the distress in the great golden eyes. "What is the complaint, Carl-my-friend?" he trilled. His accent was indescribable, but made English a sound of beauty.

"Blind luck some hysterical type didn't decide your people attacked Earth, bust in and shoot you," Donnan told him.

The man felt collected enough now to stuff and light a pipe. Through the smoke veil, he considered the Monwaingi. Yeh, he thought, they're for sure prettier than humans, but you have to see them to realize it. In words, they sound like cartoon figures. About five feet tall, the short avian body was balanced on two stout yellow legs. (The clawed toes could deal a murderous kick, Donnan had observed; the Monwaingi were perhaps more civilized than man, but there was nothing Aunt Nelly about them.) The arms, thinner and weaker than human, ended in hands whose three fingers, four-jointed and mutually opposed, were surprisingly dextrous. The head, atop a long thick neck, was large and round with a hooked beak. A throat pouch produced a whole orchestra of sounds, even labials. There was a serene grace in Ramri's form and stance; the Greeks would have liked to sculpture him. (Athens went down into a pit of fire.) But all you could really convey in words was the intense blueness of the feathers, the white plumage of tail and crest. Ramri didn't wear anything but a pouch hung from the neck, nor did he need clothes.

He plucked at the thong, miserable, looked towards Donnan and away. "I heard somewhat," he began. His tone died out in a sigh like violins. "I am so grieved." He leaned an arm on the bulkhead and his forearm on the arm, as a man might. "What can I say? I cannot even comprehend it."

Donnan started to pace, back and forth, back and forth. "You got no idea, then, what might have happened?"

"No. Certainly not. I swear—"

"Never mind, I believe you. What usually causes this sort of thing?"

Ramri pulled his face around to give Donnan a blank look. "Causes it? I do not snatch your meaning."

"How do other planets get destroyed?" Donnan barked.

"They don't."

"Huh?" Donnan stopped short. "You mean . . . no. In all the war and politicking and general hooraw throughout the galaxy—it's got to happen sometimes."

"No. Never to my knowledge. Perhaps occasionally. Who can know everything that occurs? But never in our purview of history. Did you imagine—Carl-my-friend, did you imagine my Society, any Society of Monwaing, would have introduced a planet to such a hazard? A . . . *sumdau thaungwa*—a world?" Ramri cried. "An intelligent species? An entire destiny?"

He staggered back to his framework and collapsed. A low keening began in his throat and rose, while he rocked in the seat, until the cabin rang. Even through the alien tone scale, Donnan sensed such mourning that his flesh crawled. "Stop that!" he said, but Ramri didn't seem to hear.

Was this the Monwaingi form of tears? He didn't know. There was so bloody much the human race didn't know.

And never would, probably.

Donnan beat one fist against the bulkhead. It was coming home to him too, forcing its way past every barrier he could erect, the full understanding of what had been done. Maybe so far he'd been saved from shivering into pieces by the habit of years, tight situations, violence, and death from New Mexico to New Guinea, Morocco to the Moon—and beyond—but habit was now crumpling in him too and presently he'd ram the pistol barrel up his mouth.

Or maybe, a remote part of him thought, he'd had less to lose than men like Goldspring and Wright. No wife waiting in a house they'd once painted together, no small tangletops asking for a story, not even a dog any more. There'd been girls here and there, of course. And Alison. But she'd quit and gone to Reno, and looking back long afterwards he'd understood the blame was mostly his fiddlefooted own . . . and, returning from three years among strange suns, he had daydreamed of finding someone else and making a really honest try with her. But as the barriers came down, he saw there would be no second chance, not ever again, and he started to break as other men on the ship had broken.

Until suddenly he realized he was feeling sorry

for himself. His father had taught him that was the lowest emotion a man could have. If nothing else, the impoverished rancher had given this to his son. (No, much more: horses and keen sunlight, sagebrush and blue distances and a Navajo cowboy who showed him how to stalk antelope—but all those things were vapours, adrift above growling emptiness.) The pipestem broke between Donnan's teeth. He knocked the bowl out most carefully and said:

"*Someone* did the job, I reckon. Not too long ago, either. Assuming only the superficial rocks were melted and the oceans didn't boil clear down to the bottom, it shouldn't take more than several months to cool as far as our bolometers indicate. Eh? So what's been going on in this neck of the galaxy while we were away? Guess, Ramri. You'd be more at home with interstellar politics than any human. Could the Kandemir-Vorlak war have reached this far?"

The Monwaing cut off his dirge as if with a knife. "I do not know," he said in a thin voice, like a hurt child. (Oh, God-who-doesn't-give-a-hoot, the children never knew, did they? The end came too fast for them to feel, didn't it?) "I do not believe so. And in any event . . . would even Kandemir have been so . . . *pagaung* . . . and why? What could anyone gain? Planets have sometimes been bombarded into submission, but never—" He sprang to his feet. "We did not know, we of Monwaing!" he stammered. "When we discovered Earth, twenty years ago—when we began trading and you began learning and, and, and—we never dreamed this could happen!"

"Sure," said Donnan softly. He went over and took the avian in his arms. The beaked, crested head rested on the man's breast and the body shuddered. Donnan felt the panic of total horror recede in himself. Someone aboard this bolt-bucket has to keep off his beam-ends for a while yet, he thought. I reckon I can. Try, anyway.

"Hell, Ramri," he murmured, "men have lived with more or less this possibility since they touched off their first atomic bomb, and that was—when? Sixty, seventy years ago? Something like that. Since before I was born. So finally it's happened. But thanks to you, we had spaceships when it did. A few. There must be a few other Earth ships knocking around in the galaxy. Russian, Chinese . . . they say at least one of those was co-educational. The Europeans were building two when the *Franklin* left. There was talk of crewing one with women. Damnation, chum, maybe we'd all be finished, in one of our home-grown wars, if your people hadn't showed up. Maybe you've given us a chance yet. Anyhow, you Monwaingi weren't the only ones in space. Somebody from Kandemir or Vorlak or some other planet would have dropped in on Sol within a few years if you hadn't. Galactic civilization was spreading into this spiral arm, that's all. Now come on, wipe your eyes or blow your nose or twiddle your fingers or whatever your people do. We've got work ahead of us."

He felt the warmth—the Monwaingi had a

higher body temperature than his—steal into him, as if he drew strength from this being. Ramri was viviparous, but had been nursed on food regurgitated by his parents; he breathed oxygen, but the proteins of his body were dextro-rotatory where Donnan's were laevo-rotary; he could live in a terrestroid ecology, but only after he had been immunized against dozens of different allergens; he came from a technologically advanced planet, but the concepts of his civilization could hardly be put into human terms. And yet, Donnan thought, we aren't so different in what matters.

Or are we?

He didn't let himself stiffen, outwardly, but he stood for a while weighing the possibility in a mind turned cold. And then the siren blew again, and Strathey's voice filled the ship: "Battle stations! Prepare for combat! Three unidentified objects approaching, six o'clock low. They seem to be nuclear missiles. Stand by for evasive action and combat!"

II

It is the business of the future to be dangerous.
                                           —*Whitehead*

RAMRI WAS OUT of the door before the announcement was repeated. Though human space pilots were competent enough, there was as yet none who had grown up with ships, like him and his fathers through the past century and a half. The thousand subtleties of tradition were lacking. In an emergency, Ramri took the control board.

Donnan stared after him, wrestled with temptation, and lost. He, a plain and civilian merchanical engineer, had no right to be on the bridge. But what he'd lately seen there made him doubt if anyone else did either. Not that he figured himself for a saviour; he just wanted to be

15

dealt in. With a shrug, he started after the Monwaingi.

They didn't notice him, where he stopped by the door. Ramri had taken over the main pilot chair, a convertible one adjusted to his build. Captain Strathey and Goldspring, the detector officer—apparently recovered from the initial shock—flanked him. Bowman stood near the middle of the room, prepared to go where needed. A good bunch of boys, Donnan thought. A threat to their lives was the best therapy for this moment anyone could have offered them.

His eyes searched the ports. Earth had already shrunk to view, the horror was not visible, but the cool deep-blue colour he remembered from three years ago was now greyish white, sunlight reflected off stormclouds. Luna hung near, a pearl, unchanged and unchangeable. Off to one side, its radiance stopped down by the screen, the sun disc burned within outspread wings of zodiacal light. And beyond and around lay space, totally black, totally immense, bestrewn with a million wintry stars. He realized with a shudder how little difference Ragnarok had made.

But where were the missiles? Goldspring, hunched over his instruments, was sensing them by radar and nuclear emission and the paragravitic pulses of their engines. They should have approached faster than this. The lumbering *Franklin* could not possibly out-accelerate a boat whose only payload was a hydrogen warhead.

"Yes, three, I make it," Goldspring said tonelessly. "When can we go into superlight?"

"Not soon," Ramri answered. "The nearest interference fringe must be several A.U. from here." He didn't need to calculate with the long formulas involved; a glance at Sol, an estimate of fluctuation periods, and he knew. "I suggest we—yes—"

"Don't suggest," said Strathey tightly. "Order."

"Very well, friend," The Monwaingi voice sang a string of figures. Three-fingered hands danced over the keyboard. A set of specialized computers flashed the numbers he asked for. He threw a strong vector on the ship's path and, at the proper instant, released a torpedo broadside with proper velocities.

Donnan sensed nothing except the shift in star views, until a small, brilliant spark flared and died sternward. "By the Lord Harry, we got one!" Goldspring exclaimed.

We shouldn't have, Donnan thought. Space missiles should be able to dodge better than that.

The ship thrummed. "I believe our chance of hitting the other two will improve if we let them come nearer," Ramri said. "They are now on a course only five degrees off our own; relative acceleration is low."

"How did they detect us, anyway?" Bowman asked.

'The same way we detected them," Goldspring answered. "Kept instruments wide open. Only *they* are set to home on any ship they spot."

"Sure, sure. I just wondered . . . I was off the bridge for a while. . . . Was radio silence broken? Or—" Bowman wiped his brow. It glittered with sweat, under the cold fluorescent panels.

"Certainly not!" Strathey clipped.

An idea nudged Donnan. He cleared his throat and stepped forward. The exec gaped at him, but left Strathey to roar: "What are you doing here? I'll have you in irons for this."

"Had a notion, sir," Donnan told him. "Here we got a chance to learn something. And at no extra risk, since we've already been spotted."

The captain's face writhed. Red and white chased each other across his cheeks. Then something seemed to drain from him. He slumped in his chair and muttered. "What is it?"

"Throw 'em a radio signal and see if they respond."

"They're not boats with crews aboard," Goldspring protested. "Our receivers have been kept open. Boats would have called us."

"Sure, sure. I was just wondering if those critters were set to home on radio as well as mass and engine radiation."

Goldspring looked hard at Donnan. The detector officer was a tall man, barely on the plump side, with bearded fleshy features that had been good-humoured. Now his eyes stared from black circles. He had had a family too, on Earth.

Suddenly, decisively, he touched the transmitter controls. The blips on his radar screen, the needles on other detection instruments, and the three-dimensional graph in the data summary box, all wavered before firming again. Donnan, who had come close to watch, nodded. "Yep," he said. "Thought so."

Given the additional stimulus of a radio signal,

the blind idiot brains guiding the missiles had reacted. So powerful were the engines driving those weapons that the reaction had showed as a detectable slight change of path, even at these velocities. Then the missile computers decided that the radio source was identical with the object which they were attacking, and resumed pursuit.

"Yes," Ramri said gravely, "they are programmed to destroy communicators as well as ships. In a word, anything and everything in the neighborhood that does not give them a certain signal. . . . Stand by! Fire Nine, Eight, Seven on countdown." He rattled off co-ordinates and accelerations. Elsewhere in the ship, the torpedomen adjusted their weapons, a task too intricate to be handled directly from the bridge, "Five, four, three, two, one, zero!"

The torps sprang forth. At once Ramri hauled back on his controls. Even a paragrav craft could not manoeuvre like an an airplane, but he did his best, cramming force into an orthogonal vector until Donnan heard an abused framework groan. Flame bloomed, not a hundred miles away. The screens went temporarily black at that monstrous overload. As they returned to life, the third missile passed within yards.

There was time for men to glimpse the lean shape, time even for Strathey to press a camera button. Then it had vanished. Donnan exhaled in a gust. That had been too close for comfort.

He stared at the dispersing gas cloud where the torpedoes had nailed the second missile. The incandescent wisp was quickly gulped by surrounding darkness. Goldspring nodded at his instruments. "Number Three'll be back shortly, when it's braked the speed it's got."

"I'm surprised it didn't come closer," Donnan remarked. Keep this impersonal, he thought, keep it a problem in ballistics, don't imagine the consequences if that thing zeroes in on us. No use thinking about those consequences, anyway. You'd never feel them.

"I am also," Rami declared. "I was not overly hopeful of our escaping. This ship is not designed for combat. Whoever programmed those missiles did a poor job."

"Did a good enough job on Earth," Bowman grated.

"Shut up!" Strathey's voice was very quiet.

"Stand by," Ramri's orders trilled forth. A final time, nuclei burst in space . . . so close that Donnan felt the gases buffet the *Franklin*, like a shock through his feet and into his bones, a clang and rattle that slowly toned itself away.

"Whew!" He shook his head, trying to clear it.

"How much radiation did we get that time?" Strathey asked.

"Does that matter?" Bowman replied, high-pitched and with a giggle. "We're none of us married."

Goldspring jerked in his seat. His eyes closed and he gripped the chair arms till his knuckles whitened. The viewscreen crowned his head with stars.

"Be quiet." Strathey's nostrils twitched. "Be quiet or I'll kill you."

"I'm s-sorry," Bowman stuttered. "I only—I mean—"

"Be quiet, I said!"

Goldspring relaxed like a sack of meal. "Forget it," he mumbled. "Not enough radiation to matter. The force screens can block a lot more than that." He went to work resetting his detectors.

Ramri extended one thin hand. "Let me see the pictures you took, if your pleasure be so," he requested. Strathey didn't seem to hear. Donnan brought the self-developing film out. One frame was pretty clear, even showing details of the missile's drive coils.

Ramri stared at it a long while. The stillness grew and grew.

"Recognize the make?" Donnan inquired at last.

"Yes," Ramri breathed. "I believe so." He mumbled something in his own language. "Even of them," he added, "I hate to believe this."

"Kandemir?"

"Yes. A Kandemirian Mark IV Quester. I have inspected some that were obtained by the Monwaingi intelligence service. They are standard anti-ship missiles."

"Kandemir," Strathey whispered. "My God—"

"Wait a bit, skipper," Donnan urged. "Let's not jump to conclusions."

"But—"

"Look, sir, everything I've read and heard suggests to me that those missiles ought to have wiped us out. They should've dodged everything we could throw at them and hit us broadside on. We aren't a warship; our armament was for swank, and because the Pentagon insisted a ship headed into unknown parts of the galaxy should have some weapons. Ramri, you were puzzled too, weren't you, by our escape?"

"What is your meaning, Carl-my-friend?" The troubled golden eyes searched Donnan's whole posture.

The engineer shrugged. "Damn if I know. But I would expect a Kandemirian to do a better job of adjustment on his own machines. Mainly, though, I'd like to forestall any notion you guys may have got about heading straight for Kandemir and doing a kamikaze dive on to their main city."

"They don't have a main city." Bowman giggled again.

Goldspring glanced about. "I've just spotted several more objects approaching," he said. "They're still at the limits of detection, so I can't positively identify their type. But what else would they be except missiles?"

Donnan nodded. "The whole Solar System must be lousy with missiles in orbit."

"We cannot linger here, then," Ramri said. "To a certain extent, only a fortunate concatenation of initial vectors allowed us to stand off the first three, poorly self-guided though they were. The second attack, or the third, will surely destroy us." He considered the instrument readings. "However, we should certainly be able to reach the nearest interference fringe ahead of that flock. Once we go superlight, we will be safe."

From everything except ourselves, Donnan thought.

"Get going, then," Strathey rapped.

Ramri busied himself with computation and thereafter with piloting. The humans eased a trifle, lit cigarettes, worked arms and legs to get some of the tension out. They were all shockingly haggard, Donnan observed; he wondered if he looked so corpse-like. But they were able to talk rationally.

"Did Kunz find what happened to our artificial Earth satellites?" he asked. "The observations and moon relays and so on?"

"Gone," Strathey said. He gagged. "Also the Moon bases. A new crater where each base had been."

"Yeh, I reckon we had to expect that." Donnan sighed. McGee, assistant powerman at U.S.A.-Tycho, had been a particular friend of his. He remembered one evening when they got drunk and composed *The Ballad of Superintendent Ball*, whose scurrilous verses were presently being sung throughout the space service. And now McGee and Ball were both dead, and Donnan was signed on the Flying Dutchman. Well-a-day.

"Kunz and I tried to detect any trace of life," Goldspring said. "Not human . . . no such hope . . . but a ship or a base or anything of the enemy's—" His words faded out.

"No luck, eh? Wouldn't've expected it, myself," Donnan said. "Whoever murdered Earth had no reason to hang around. He'll let his missiles destroy anyone who comes snooping. Later on, at his leisure, he can come back here himself and do whatever he figures on."

Ramri turned around long enough to say harshly, "He would not wish his identity known. I tell you, no one has committed such an atrocity before. The whole galaxy will rise to crush Kandemir."

"If Kandemir is guilty," Donnan said. His shoulders slumped. "Anyhow, the whole galaxy will do no such thing. The whole galaxy will never hear about this incident. A few dozen planets in our local spiral arm may be shocked—but I wonder if they'll take action. What's Earth to them?"

"If nothing else," Ramri said, "they will wish to prevent any such thing being done to their own selves."

"How was it done, do you think?" Bowman asked wearily.

"Several multi-gigaton disruption bombs, fired simultaneously, would serve." Ramri's tone was the bleakest sound Donnan had ever heard. "The operation would require a small task force—each bomb is the size of a respectable asteroid—but still, the undertaking was not too big to be clandestine. The energy of the bombs would be released primarily as shock waves in crust and mantle, which, in turn, would become heat. There would be little residual radioactivity. . . . No, I beg you, I cannot talk further of this at present." As he faced back to the pilot board, he began keening, very low.

After a while Captain Strathey said, "We had better proceed to some habitable planet of a nearby star, such as Tau Ceti II. Any other surviving ships can join us there."

"How'd they know where to look?" Donnan asked. "There are hundreds of possibilities within easy range. And besides, for all they know, we'll've hightailed it to the opposite end of the galaxy."

"True. I thought at first we could pick some definite star to go to and place a radio transmitter, broadcasting a recording of our whereabouts, in orbit around the Earth. Now that's obviously ruled out. Even if we could stop to make such a satellite, the missiles would destroy it."

"They'll also endanger any ship which returns here," Goldspring pointed out. "Our escape was indeed partly luck. The next people might not be so fortunate. We've got to do more than get word to the others where to find us. We've got to warn them not to return to the Solar System in the first place."

"Are there any others?" Bowman cried. "Maybe they've all come back and been wiped out. Maybe we're the last humans alive—" He clamped his jaws. His fingers twisted together.

"Maybe," said Donnan. "However, don't forget that several expeditions were a-planning at the time we left. We and the Russians had completed our big ships first, but China and the British Commonwealth had almost finished theirs and the Europeans expected to do so within another year. Of course, we don't know where any of 'em went. The Russkies and Chinese wouldn't say a meaningful word; the British and Europeans still hadn't made up their minds; and then some other countries like India might have gone ahead and started spacing too, that weren't figuring on it three years back. Sure, perhaps everybody else made short hops and got home before us and died with Earth. But I sort of doubt that. Humans had already visited a good deal of the local territory, as passengers on other planets' ships. There'd be small glory in repeating such a trip. Better go some place new."

Like us, he thought, running headlong towards Sagittarius and the star clouds at galactic centre. Doubtless we weren't the first. Among the millions of space-faring races, we can't have been the first to look at the galaxy's heart, and curve up to look at the entire beautiful sight, and gather enough data to keep our scientists happy for the next hundred years. But none of our neighbor peoples had done so, even though they had spaceships before we did. They aren't that kind. They accepted space travel when it came to them, and traded and discovered and had adventures, and in the course of time they'd have got around to stunts like ours. But man had to go look first of all for God. And fail, naturally. Man is a nut from way back. The galaxy will miss a lot of fun, now he's gone.

He is not. I say he is not.

"Assume other Terrestrial ships are kicking around then," Goldspring said with a humourless chuckle. "Assume, even, that they come home like us and escape again like us. Have *we* any idea where *they* will go?"

"Local habitable planets," Strathey said. "That makes sense."

"Uh-uh." Donnan shook his head. "How do you know the enemy isn't there too? Or, at least, won't come hunting there for just such remnants as us?"

The idea rammed home and they stared at each other. Donnan went on: "Anyhow, we know already, from information given us by non-humans and from expeditions of our own on chartered foreign ships . . . we know that the nearest terrestroid planets are pretty miserable places. At best, you'll find yourself in a jungle, with gibbering stone-age natives for company. We aren't set up for that. Three hundred men would be so busy surviving they wouldn't have time to think."

"What do you propose instead?" None thought it strange that Strathey should ask the question.

"Well, I'd say go beyond this immediate vicinity, on to some place civilized. Some place with a decent climate. Most especially, some place where facilities are available. Why be second-rate Robinson Crusoes when we are first-rate technicians . . . and can get good jobs on the strength of that? Also, we'll be in a better position to hear any news of other ships like ours."

"Y-yes. Quite correct. I do think we should stop at Tau Ceti, perhaps one or two other local stars, and leave radio satellites. I admit the sheer number of such stars makes it improbable that any other survivors will come upon our message, but the time and effort we lose making the attempt will not be great. Thereafter, though . . . yes, I agree. One of the clusters of civilization, where numerous planets practice space travel."

"Which one?" Goldspring asked. "I've seen the estimate that there are a million such in the entire galaxy."

"Our own, of course," Ramri said over his shoulder. "The cluster of Monwaing and its colonies, Vorlak, Yann, Xo—"

"And Kandemir and its empire," Strathey reminded.

"Not to Kandemir, certainly," Ramri said. "But you must go to a Monwaingi world. Where else? You will be made welcome in any of our cultures. My own Tanthai on Katkinu in particular—but Monwaing itself would also—"

"No," Bowman interrupted.

"What?" Ramri blinked at him. The throat pouch quivered.

"No," repeated Bowman. "Not Monwaing or its colonies. Not till we know Monwaing isn't the one that destroyed Earth!"

III

The horror of the human condition—any human condition—is that one soon grows used to it.

—Sanders

TAU CETI II was no place for a stroll. Safe enough, but there was nothing to see except a few thorn-plants straggling across rusty dunes, under a glaring reddish sun. The air was hot and dry and so charged with carbon dioxide that it felt perpetually stuffy. This was in the sub-arctic Camp Jeffers region, of course, explored by Australians in a chartered Vorlakka ship ten years ago. The rest of the planet was worse.

Nevertheless, after forty-eight hours in camp, Donnan had to get away or go crazy. He and Arnold Goldspring loaded their packboards and started off. No use asking the captain's permission. Strathey was disintegrating as fast as his crew, and it was becoming a rabble.

"Makes no sense to land in the first place," Donnan had grumbled. "They talk about a rest after being cooped in the ship. Hell, they'll be more cooped in a bunch of tents down there, and a lot less comfortable. All we want to do is make an orbital satellite and leave a radio note in it . . . once we've decided where we want to go from here."

"I said as much to the crew committee," the captain answered. He wouldn't meet the engineer's eyes. "They insisted. I can't risk mutiny."

"Huh? You're the skipper, aren't you?"

"I'm a Navy man, Mr. Donnan. The personnel aboard are seventy-five per cent civilians."

"What's that got to do with anything?"

"That's enough!" Strathey said, raw-voiced. "Get out of here."

Donnan got. But from then on he carried his gun in a shoulder holster beneath his coverall.

Endless, hysterical debate reached no decision on what to say in the recording. Should the *Franklin* find some primitive world, a safe hiding place . . . safe, also, from discovery by any other humans that might still be alive and looking for their kindred? Go to a planet in this nucleus of civilization? If so, which planet—when any might be the secret enemy? (Ramri now had two marines as a permanent guard. They had already had to discourage a few men who said no filthy alien was fit to live. But they were his jailers as well; everyone understood that, even if no one came right out and said so.) Or ought the *Franklin* to go across thousands of light-years to an altogether different group of space-faring peoples? That wouldn't be too long a trip for her. But the sheer numbers of such clusters and the thinness of contact between them would make it unlikely that other humans searching at random would ever come upon word of the Americans.

As the shrillness mounted, Donnan finally said to hell with it and left camp.

Goldspring would once have been a cheerful companion. He had been throughout the past three years, on scores of worlds. (Including a certain uncharted one, lonely and beautiful, almost another Earth, which they had excitedly discussed as a future colony. But that was before they came home.) Now he was sunk in moodiness. He spent his abundant free time among books and papers, making esoteric calculations. The work was an escape for him, Donnan knew; the Goldsprings had been a close-knit family. But when he began shaking so badly that he spilled half his food at mess, Donnan decided something else was indicated. He persuaded Goldspring to come along on the hike.

Eventually, one night under two hurtling moons, Goldspring cracked open. What he said was mostly reminiscence, and no one else's business. Donnan helped him through the spell as best he could. Thereafter Goldspring felt better. They started walking back.

It was good to have someone to talk with again. "What's this project of yours, Arn?" Donnan asked conversationally. "All the figuring you've been doing?"

"A theoretical notion." Like most of the ship's personnel, Goldspring was a scientist rather than a career spaceman. His specialty was field physics, and his doubling in brass as detector officer was incidental.

He tilted back his hat to mop his forehead. The nearby sun glowered on them, two specks in a rolling red immensity. Puffs of dust marked every step they made. The air shimmered. Nothing else moved.

"Yeh?" Donnan hitched his pack to a more comfortable position. "Can you put it in words a plain M.E. can understand?"

"I don't know. How familiar are you, really, with the concept the superlight drive is based on? The mathematical depiction of space as having a structure equivalent to a set of standing waves in an n-dimensional continuum."

"Well, I've read some of the popular accounts. Let's see if I remember. Where these waves interfere, you can slip from one to another. Out between the stars, where there isn't much gravitational distortion, the interference fringes come so close together that instead of taking the entire straight-line distance, as light does, you can skip most of it. The whole business is the other side of the galactic-recession phenomenon. Galaxies recede from each other because space is generated between them. A ship in superlight brings the stars closer, in effect, by using those zones where space is being cancelled out. Have I got it straight?"

Goldspring winced. "Never mind. I'm sorry I asked." For a time there was only the scrunch of their boots in sand. Then he shrugged. "Let's just say the possibility occurred to me of inverting the effect. Instead of passing a material object through the fringes, keep the object still and make it generate fringes artificially. Oh, not on anything like the cosmic scale. We haven't the mass or energy to affect more than a few thousand kilometres of radius. However, the result should be measurable. So far, developing the idea, I haven't seen any holes in my reasoning. I'd like to make an experimental test as soon as possible."

"Don't bother," Donnan said. "Look up the results in some scientific journal. Surely, in the thousands of years that there's been space travel, somebody else thought of this."

"No doubt," said Goldspring. "But not any local scientists. And by local I don't mean just this immediate civilization cluster, but everything within ten thousand light-years. I've studied a lot of non-human texts, both in translation and—in Tantha and Uru, anyhow—in the original. M.I.T. had quite a file of such books and journals. Nowhere have I seen mention of any such phenomenon.

"Besides," he added, "the applications would be so revolutionary that if the effect were known (assuming it really exists, of course!), we'd be using a lot different machines for a lot different purposes."

"Whoa! What a minute," Donnan objected. "That doesn't make sense. The Monwaingi discovered the Earth only twenty years ago. Three years back, the first Earth-built spaceships were finally completed. Monwaing itself was discovered something like a hundred and fifty years ago. And the ships that started up modern civilization there were from a planet that'd been exploring space for God knows how many centuries. D'you mean to tell me a bunch of newcomers like us can show the galaxy something it hasn't known since our ancestors were hunting mammoths?"

"I do," said Goldspring. "Don't confuse science with technology. Most intelligent species that man's encountered to date don't think along identical lines with man. Why should they? Different biology, different home environment, different culture and history. Look what happened on Earth whenever two societies met. The more backward one would try to modernize, but it never quite became a carbon copy of the other. Compare the different versions of Christianity that evolved as Christianity spread through Europe; think of the ingenious new wrinkles in science and industry that the Japanese developed after they decided to industrialize. And that involved strictly human beings. The tendency towards parallel development is still weaker between wholly distinct species. Do you think we could ever . . . could ever have borrowed the Monwaingi concept of the nation as a mere framework for radically different civilizations to grow in? Or that we'd ever have had any reason, economic or otherwise, to develop pure bio-technics as far as them?"

"Okay, Arn, okay. But still—"

"No, let me finish. On Earth we seemed rather slow to assimilate the technology of galactic civilization. That's highly understandable. We had to find ways of attracting out-world traders, develop stuff they wanted, so that we in exchange could buy books and machines, get scholarships for our bright young men, rent spaceships for our own initial ventures. Our being divided into rival nations didn't help us, either. And the sheer job of tooling up required time. I'll give you an analogy. Suppose some imaginary time traveller from around the year you were born had gone back to . . . oh, say 1930 . . . and told the General Electric researchers of that time about transistors. It'd have taken those boys years to develop the necessary auxiliary machines, and develop the necessary skills, to use the information. They'd have to make up a quarter century of progress in a dozen allied arts. And—there wouldn't have been any initial demand for transistors. No apparatus in use in 1930 demanded such miniature electronic valves. The very need—the market— would have had to be slowly created."

"Shucks, I know that. I am an engineer, they tell me."

"But my point is," Goldspring said, "there would not have been any corresponding difficulty in assimilating the theory of the transistor. Any good physicist could have learned everything about solid-state phenomena in a few months. All he'd need would be the texts and a few instruments.

"Likewise, when the Monwaingi came, Terrestrial science leap-frogged a thousand years or more, almost overnight. Terrestrial technology was what lagged. And not by much, at that. Ramri often remarked to me how astonished he was at our rate of modernization."

"Okay, then, I concede," Donnan said. "I'll assume you brought a fresh viewpoint to this interference fringe subject and really have stumbled on to something that none of our neighbours ever thought of. But you can't make me believe that in the entire galaxy, throughout its history, you are unique."

"Oh, no, certainly not. My discovery (if, I repeat, it is a discovery and not a blind alley) must have been duplicated hundreds of times. It just didn't happen to have been duplicated locally. And the knowledge hasn't spread into our part of the galaxy. That's not surprising either. Who could keep up with a fraction of the intellectual activity on several million civilized planets? Why, I'll bet there are a billion professional journals—or equivalent thereof—published every day."

"Yeah." Donnan smiled rather sadly. "Y'know," he remarked, "when I was a kid in my teens, just before the Monwaingi came, I went on a science fiction kick. I must've read hundreds of stories where there were races travelling between the stars while humans had barely reached the nearer planets of their own system. But I can't recall one that ever guessed the truth—the bloody simple obvious truth of the case. Always, if the Galactics noticed us, they were benevolent secret guardians; or not-so-benevolent keepers; or kept strictly hands off. In some stories they did land openly, as the Monwaingi and the rest actually did. But as near as I remember, in the stories this was always a prelude to inviting Earth into the Galactic Federation.

"Hell, why should there be a Federation? Why should anyone give a hoot about us? Couldn't those writers see how *big* the universe is?"

—Big indeed. The diameter of this one galaxy is some hundred thousand light-years, the maximum width about ten thousand. It includes on the order of a hundred billion stars, at least half of which have at least one life-bearing planet. A goodly percentage of these latter also sustain intelligent life.

Sol lies approximately thirty thousand light-years from galactic centre, where the stars begin to thin out towards emptiness: a frontier region, which the most rapidly expanding civilization of space travellers would still be slow to reach. And no such civilization could expand rapidly anyhow. There are too many stars.

At some unknown time in some unknown place, someone created the first superlight spaceship. Or perhaps it was created independently, many times and places. No one knows. Probably no one will ever know; there are too many archives in too many languages to search. But in any event the explorers went forth. They visited, studied, mapped, traded. Most of the races they found were primitive—or, if civilized, were not interested in space travel for themselves. Some few had the proper degree of industrialization and the proper attitude of outwardness. They learned from the explorers. Why should they not? The explorers had nothing to fear from these strangers, who paid them well for instruction. There is plenty of room in space. Besides, a complete planet is self-sufficient, both economically and politically.

From these newly awakened worlds, then, a second generation of explorers went forth. They had to go farther than the first; planets of interest to them lay far, far away, lost in a wilderness of suns whose worlds were barren, or savage, or too foreign for intercourse. But eventually someone, at an enormous distance from their home, learned space technology in turn from them.

Thus the knowledge radiated, through millennia, but not like a wave of light from a single candle. Rather it spread like dandelion seeds, blown at random, each seed which takes root begetting a cluster of offspring. A newly civilized planet (by that time, "civilization" was equated in the minds of space-farers with the ability to travel through space) would occupy itself with its nearer neighbours. Occasionally there was contact with one of the other loose astro-politico-economic clumps. But the contact was sporadic.

There was no economic force to maintain it, and, culturally, these clusters diverged too much.

And once in a while, some daring armada— traders looking for a profit, explorers looking for knowledge, refugees looking for a home, or persons with motives less comprehensible to a human—would make the big jump and start yet another nucleus of civilization.

Within each such nucleus, a certain unity prevailed. There was trading; for, while no planet had to supply another with necessities, the materials of comfort, luxury, amusement, and research were in demand. There was tourism. There was a degree of interchange in science, art, religion, fashion. Sometimes there was war.

But beyond the nucleus, the cluster, there was little or nothing. No mind could possibly deal with all the planets in space. The number was so huge. A space-faring people must needs confine serious attention to their own vicinity, with infrequent small ventures beyond. Anything more would have been impossible. The civilization-clusters were never hostile to each other. There was nothing to be hostile about. Conflicts occurred among neighbours, not among strangers who saw each other once a year, a decade, or a century.

Higgledy-piggledy, helter-skelter, civilization spread out among the stars. A million clusters, comprising one to a hundred planets each, furnished the only pattern there was. Between the clusters as wholes, no pattern whatsoever existed. A spaceship could cross the galaxy in months;

but a news item, if sensational enough to make the journey at all, might take a hundred years.

There was little enough pattern within any given cluster. It was no more than a set of planets, not too widely separated, which maintained some degree of fairly regular contact with each other. These planets might have their own colonies, dependencies, or newly discovered spheres of influence, as Earth had been for Monwaing. But there was no question of a single culture for the whole cluster, or any sort of overall government. And never forget: any planet is a world, as complex and mysterious in its own right, as full of its own patterns and contradictions and histories, as ever Earth was.

No wonder the speculative writers had misunderstood their own assumptions. The universe was too big for them—

Donnan shook himself and forced his mind back to practicalities. "Think we might find some use for this prospective gadget of yours?" he asked.

"For a whole series of gadgets, you mean," Goldspring said. "Sure. That was why I tackled the math so hard after . . . after we came back and saw. If we aren't simply to become a bunch of hirelings, we'll need something special to sell." He paused. One hand went to his beard and tugged until the physical pain outweighed what was within. "Also," he said, "one day we'll know who killed eight billion human beings. I don't think whoever that was should go unpunished."

"You'll vote, then, to stay in this local cluster?

The guilty party must belong to it. Nobody from another cluster would mount a naval operation like that. Too far; no reason to."

"That's obvious." Goldspring nodded jerkily. "And out of the planets that even knew Earth existed, there are really only three possible suspects. Kandemir, Vorlak, and the Monwaing complex. The last two don't make sense either." He bit his lip. "But what does, in this universe?"

"I'll buck for sticking around myself," Donnan agreed, "though I got a kind of different reason. You see—Hullo, there's the end of our stroll."

They had mounted a high dune overlooking the sheltered valley in which the men had pitched camp. Even from this distance the tents around the upright spears of the auxiliary boats looked slovenly. A dust cloud hung in the air above. A lot of movement, to raise that much. . . . Donnan broke out his field glasses. He stared for so long that Goldspring began to fidget. When he lowered them, the physicist snatched them while Donnan's mouth formed a soundless whistle.

"I don't understand," Goldspring said. "Looks like an assembly. Everyone seems to be gathered near Boat One. But—"

"But they're boiling around like ants whose nest was just stove in," Donnan snapped. "Seems as if we got back barely in time. Come on!"

His stocky form broke into jogtrot. Goldspring braced himself and followed. For the next few miles they made no sound but footfalls and harshening breath.

The camp was near riot when they arrived.

Three hundred men surged and yelled around the lead boat. Its passenger lock, high in the bows, stood open. The gang-ladder had been partially extended to form a rostrum, where Lieutenant Howard, the second mate, jittered among a squad of marines. Now and then he fumbled at a microphone. But the P.A. only amplified his stutters and the growling and shouting on the ground soon overwhelmed him. The marines stood alert, rifles ready. Under the overshadowing battle helmets, their faces looked white and very young.

Men clamoured. Men talked to their fellows, argued, shouted, stamped off in a rage or struck blows which drew blood. Here and there a man who happened to have a gun stood as a sullen shield for a few of the timid. Two corpses sprawled near a tent. One had been shot. The other was too badly trampled for Donnan to be sure what had happened. Occasionally, above the hubbub, a pistol cracked. Warning shots only, Donnan hoped.

"What's going on?" Goldspring groaned. "What's happened, Carl—in God's name—"

Donnan stopped before a clump of peaceful men. He recognized them as scientists and technicians, mostly huddled together, eyes glassy with shock. Their guardian was the planetographer Easterling, who had found an automatic rifle somewhere. He poked the muzzle in Donnan's direction. "Move along," he rapped. "We don't want any trouble."

"Nor me, Sam." Donnan kept hands well away

from his own pistol. "I just returned. Been away the better part of a week, me and Arnold here. What the hell broke loose?"

Easterling lowered his weapon. He was a big young black; an ancient fear had doubled his bitterness at this violence which seethed towards explosion. But Donnan's manner eased his hostility. He had to raise his voice as a fresh babble of shouts—"Kill the swine! Kill the swine!"—broke loose from a score of men gathered some yards off. But his tone became steadier:

"Huh! No wonder you look so bug-eyed. Hell's the right word, man. All hell let out for noon. Half of 'em want to hang Yule and half of 'em want to give him a medal . . . and they're split apart on the question of where to go and what to do anyway, so this has turned arguments into fights. We had one riot a few hours back. It sputtered out when the marines beat off an attack on the boat. But now another attack's building up. When they've got enough nerve together, they'll try again to lynch Yule. Then the pro-Yules'll hit the lynchers from behind, I s'pose. Those who want to go to Monwaing and those who want to hide in some other cluster are close to blows on that difference too. Me, I hope we here can stay out of harm's way till the rest have knocked some sense into each other. Come join us, we need sober men."

"I never thought—" Goldspring covered his eyes. "The best men the whole United States could find . . . they said . . . men come to this!"

Donnan spat. "With Earth gone, and a commander whose nerve went to pieces, I'm not surprised. What touched this mob action off, Sam? Where is the captain, anyway?"

"Dead," Easterling answered flatly. "We did get the whole story this morning, before the situation went completely to pot. Seems Bowman, the exec, made a pass at Yule. Or so Yule claims. Yule tried to kill him, barehanded. Bowman had a gun, but Yule got it away from him. Captain Strathey came running to stop the fight. The gun went off. An accident, probably . . . only then Yule proceeded to shoot Bowman too, with no doubt about malice aforethought. A couple of marines jumped him—too late. He's confined in Boat One now for court-martial. Lieutenant Howard assumed command. But as the day wore on, most of the camp stopped listening to him."

"I was afraid of something like this," Donnan breathed. "Yule wasn't scared of Bowman, I'll bet; he could've said no and let the matter rest. He was scared of himself. So are a lot of those guys milling around there."

"I wish we'd all died with Earth," Goldspring choked.

"To hell with that noise," Donnan said. "Those are good men. Good, you hear? Nothing wrong with 'em except they've had the underpinnings, and props and keystones and kingposts knocked out from their lives. Strathey was the one who failed. He should have provided something new, immediately, to take up the slack and give the wound a chance to heal. Howard's failing 'em still worse. Why the blue blazes does he stand there gibbering? Why don't he take charge?"

"How?" Easterling's teeth flashed in a wolf grin.

"By not quacking at everybody but addressing himself directly to the ones like you, that he can see have got more self-control than average," Donnan said. "Organize them into an anti-riot guard. Issue clubs and tear gas bombs. Break a few heads, maybe, if he has to; but restore order before this thing gets completely out of hand. And then, stop asking them what they think we ought to do. Tell them what we're going to do."

"I think," said a man behind Easterling, very softly, "that Howard planned to get married when he came home."

"That's no excuse," Donnan replied. "Or if it is, we need somebody who doesn't make excuses."

Goldspring watched him for a long moment; and bit by bit, all their eyes swung to him. No one spoke.

Me? Donnan thought wildly. Me?

But I'm nobody. Ranch kid, tramp, merchant seaman, then an engineering degree and a bunch of jobs around the world. A few investments got me a bit of money that's now gone in smoke, and I made friends with a Senator who's now ash in the lava. I wanted badly enough to get on the *Franklin*—as what man didn't who had any salt in his blood?—that I lobbied for myself for six months. So I got an assignment, to study any interesting outplanet mechanical techniques we might happen upon. I did, on a dozen planets in four separate civilization-clusters; but anyone in my profession could have done as well. It wasn't important anyway. The *Franklin's* real purpose was to get a sketch of a beginning of a ghost of an idea of the galaxy, its layout and characteristics, beyond what we'd learned from Monwaing. And to develop American spacefaring techniques. Both of which purposes became meaningless when America sank.

Me take over? I'd only get killed trying.

Donnan wet his lips. For a moment his heartbeat drowned the mob noise. He brought the pulse under control, but he still had to husk a few times before he could say, "Okay, let's get started."

IV

O western wind, when wilt thou blow,
  That the small rain down can rain?
Christ, if my love were in my arms
  And I in my bed again!
          —*Anon. (16th century)*

As THE *EUROPA* matched vectors, the missile became visible to unaided eyes. Sigrid Holmen looked from her pilot board and saw the shark form, still kilometres away but magnified by the screen, etched against blackness and thronged stars. Her finger poised on the emergency thrust button. Something would go wrong, she told herself wildly; it would, and no human muscles could close the engine circuit fast enough for the ship to escape. To travel so far and then return to be killed!

But did that matter? herself answered in uprushing anguish. When Earth was an ember, when hills and forests were vanished, when every trace of her folk from the time they entered the land to hunt elk as the glaciers melted to the hour when Father and Mother bade her good-bye in their old red-roofed house . . . when everything was gone? One senseless kick of some cosmic boot, and the whole long story came to an end and had all been for nothing.

Hatred of the murderers crowded out fear and grief alike. Hatred focused so sharply on the thing which pursued her ship that it seemed the steel must melt.

Steadily, then, her finger rested. She watched the missile drift across her view as it checked acceleration to change course. She watched it begin to overhaul again. Still the *Europa* plodded away from dead Earth at a stolid five gravities; and still Chief Gunnery Officer Vukovic crouched immobile over her instruments, adjusting her controls. Time stretched until Sigrid felt time must rip across.

"*Bien,*" Alexandra Vukovic said, and punched a button of her own. The slugs that hosed from No. One turret were not visible, but she leaned back and reached into her shapeless uniform tunic. She even grinned a little. The pack of cigarettes was not yet out of her pocket when the slugs struck. From end to end they smote the missile. Thermite plus oxidizer seamed it with white fire. Sigrid watched the thin plates torn open, curling as if in agony. Good! she exulted. The missile dropped from view. She cut paragrav thrust and asked the radar officer, Katrina Tenbroek, for a reading. The Dutch girl forced herself out of a white-faced daze and reported the missile had ceased acceleration.

"We killed its brain, then," Alexandra Vukovic said. "As I hoped. I know we did not simply kill its engines. I took care not to strike that far aft. So the warhead is now disarmed. Well and good, we can approach."

She spoke the French that was the common language of the expedition with a strong Serbian accent, but fluently. Her wiry frame relaxed easy as a cat in the chair, and no further expression showed on her scarred face. She's tough, Sigrid thought, not for the first time. Had to be, I suppose, to fight the Russians in the "Balkan incident" of 1995 as she did. But when the whole Earth has died . . . no, it isn't human to stay that cool!

Then she noticed how raggedly Alexandra inhaled her cigarette, and how fingernails had drawn blood from the gunner's palm.

Captain Edith Poussin's voice rapped over the intercom: "Oh, no, you don't, my dears. We aren't coming near that thing. It may be booby trapped."

"But Madame!" Sigrid Holmen sat straight in astonishment. "You agreed—when we decided there was a chance to capture it for examination—I mean, what's the use, if now we won't take a look?"

"We will," said Captain Poussin. "Yes, indeed. And perhaps find out whose it is, no?" Sigrid envisaged her in the central control chamber, plump, grey, reminding one more of some Dordogne housewife than an anthropologist and xenologist with an astronautical degree from the University of Oao on Unya. But her tone was like winter, and suddenly the pilot remembered those grandmothers who had sat knitting beneath the guillotine.

"Let us not be fools," Edith Poussin continued. "Two missiles we destroyed, one we have disabled; but does that not argue they orbit in trios? I think we can expect more to come along at any moment, as they happen within detection range of us. Fortunately, we have not such a great heavy ship as the Americans or Russians do. However, speed and manoeuvrability will not save us from a mass onslaught. No, our first duty is to escape." Clipped: "I want three volunteers to make us fast to that missile and examine it while we proceed towards the nearest interference fringe. Respectively a navigation officer, weapons expert, and electronician."

Sigrid rose. She was a tall young Swede, eyes blue and Italian-cut hair yellow, her features regular without being exceptional but her form handsomer than most. On that account she chose to wear less clothing than most of the *Europa's* hundred women. But vanity had departed with Earth and hope. She was only conscious of an adrenalin tingle as she said, "That's us right here."

"Aye," said Alexandra. Katrina Tenbroek shook her head. "No," she stammered. "Please."

"Are you afraid?" scoffed the Yugoslav.

"None of that, Vukovic," the captain's voice interjected. "Apologize at once."

"Afraid?" Katrina shook her head. "What is there to be afraid of, after today? B—b—but I have to cry . . . for a while. . . . I'm sorry."

Alexandra stared at the deck. The scar on her cheek stood lividly forth. "I'm sorry too," she mumbled. "It is only that I don't dare cry." She turned on her heel.

"Wait!" Sigrid was surprised to hear herself call. "Wait till we're relieved."

Alexandra stopped. "Of course. Stupid of me. I—oh—" She smashed the butt of her cigarette and took another. Sigrid almost reminded her that there would be no more tobacco when the ship's supply was gone, not ever again, but checked the words in time.

Father, she thought. Mother. Nils. Olaf. Stockholm Castle, and sailboats among the islands, and that funny friendly little man in Lapland the year we took our vacation there. The whole Earth—I should not have studied space piloting. I should not have gone on practice cruises. That was time I could have spent with them. I should not have taken this berth. I sold my right to die with them. Oh, no, no, no, I am having a nightmare, I am insane, this cannot be. Or else God himself has gone senile and crazy. Why is the sun still shining? How does it dare?

Her relief, Herta Eisner, entered with Yael Blum and Marina Alberghetti. All three looked unnaturally relaxed. Sigrid knew why when the German extended a box of pills.

"No," Sigrid said. "I don't want to hide behind any damned chemistry."

"Take that tranquilizer," Captain Poussin called. "Everyone. That's an order. We can't afford emotions yet."

Sigrid gulped and obeyed. As she and Alexandra proceeded down the starboard corridor, she felt the drug take hold: an inward numbness, but a tautening and swiftening of the logical mind, so that ideas fairly flew across the surface. Red-haired Engineer Gertrud Hedtke of Switzerland met them at the suit locker. She pushed a paragrav barrow loaded with tools and coiled cable they would need. Wordless, they helped each other into their spacesuits and went out of the airlock.

Space gloomed and glittered around them. The sun was a fire too fierce to look at, the Milky Way an infinitely cold cataract, stars and stars filled the sky—through which, in free fall, they went endlessly tumbling. Away from the ship's background sounds, silence pressed inwards till one's own breath became a noise like an elemental force. The noise of the quern Grotte, Sigrid thought remotely, which the giantesses Fenja and Menja turn beneath the sea, which grinds forth salt and cattle and treasure, broad lands and rich harvests and spring-time dawns; which grinds forth war, bloody spears, death and burning and Fimbul Winter.

She turned her back on Grotte, scornfully, and gave her attention to the job.

The *Europa*, a slim tapered cylinder, as beautiful to see as she was to handle, had matched velocities with the missile at some four kilometres' remove. That should be safe, even if the hydrogen warhead did go off; empty space won't transmit concussion, and at that distance the screens could ward off radiant energy sufficiently well. Flitting about on paragrav units, the women attached twin cables to the king-brace amidships and paid them out on their way to the prize. Modern galactic technology was marvellous, thought Sigrid; these metal cords which could withstand fifty thousand tons of pull were no thicker than her little finger and massed no more than a hundred kilos per kilometre. But I'd rather weave a bast rope with bleeding hands, to use on a green Earth, it cried within her.

The drug suppressed the wish. She approached the missile with no fear of an explosion. Her death would be meaningless, even welcome, when Earth's children and men were dead. Quickly she helped patch the cables on, then she and Alexandra left Gertrud to make a proper weld while they both ducked into a hole burned through the shell.

Darkness inside was total. As Sigrid groped for the flash-button on her wrist, Captain Poussin's voice sounded in her helmet receiver: "Other objects detected approaching. We can outrun them at one-point-five gravities, I think. Stand by." She braced herself against the surge of weight.

Undiffused, the flashbeams were puddles of illumination which picked crowded enigmatic machinery out of night. Sigrid squirmed after Alexandra until they reached a central passageway big enough to stand in. The missile was being towed with its main axis transverse to the acceleration, so that they could walk down its length.

Gauges and switches threw back the light from a tangle of wires. A faceless troll shape in her armour, Alexandra asked low, "do you recognize any of this?"

"Kandemirian?" Sigrid hesitated. "I think so. I don't know their languages or . . . or anything . . . but once I saw their principal alphabet in a dictionary. I believe the letters and numbers looked like this." One clumsy gauntlet pointed to a meter dial.

"Give me some light and I'll photograph a sample. The Old Lady will know." Alexandra unslung the camera from her waist. "But I can tell you for certain, this missile is Kandemirian-built. They taught us what little was known about out-world military equipment at the officers' academy in Belgrade. I've seen pictures of just this type. The corridor we're in is for workmen to move around, making repairs, and for technicians to go to programme the brain. Those vermin," she added colourlessly.

"Kandemir. The nomad planet. But why would they—"

"Imperialists. They've already overrun a dozen worlds."

"But that's hundreds of light-years from here!"

"We've been gone for more than two years, Sigrid. Much could have happened." Alexandra laughed; the sound echoed in her helmet. "Much did happen. Come, let's look at the brain. That'll be towards the bow."

At the end of the passage they found the controls, what the thermite shells had left of them. Sigrid swung her light around, searching for any trace of—of what? A scrawl on the bulkhead caught her eye.

She leaned closer. "What's this?" she asked. "See here. Something scribbled in some kind of grease pencil."

"Notes to refer to, as the writer worked at programming the brain," Alexandra guessed. "Ummm . . . *sacre bleu*, I swear there are two distinct symbologies. Perhaps one is a non-Kandemirian alphabet? I'll photograph them for Madame." She busied herself. Sigrid gazed into blackness.

Gertrud came fumbling and clumping along. "Finish quickly, please," she said. "I just got a message from the ship. Still more missiles are on their way. We shall have to cast loose the tow and go at high acceleration to escape them."

"Well, I think we've got everything from this beast we need," Alexandra said.

Sigrid followed the others numbly. She did not begin to come to herself until they were back in the *Europa*.

The ship throbbed with gathering speed, outward bound, soon to go superlight and return to the stars. Earth's corpse and the hounds that guarded it receded sternwards. As their transquillizers wore off, most of the crew wept. Hysterics had been forestalled; they simply wept in quiet hopelessness.

After some hours, Captain Poussin summoned the missile party to her cabin. Walking down the corridor, Sigrid felt her eyes hot and puffed. But *I am over the worst,* she decided. *I will mourn you forever, Earth, Father and Mother, but I am no longer willing to die. For while we live, there is the hope of revenge: and infinitely more, the hope of homes and children on some new Earth where you shall never be forgotten.*

The captain's cabin was a small, comfortable, book-lined room. She sat beneath pictures of her husband, many years dead, and her sons and grandsons who must now also be dead. Her face showed little sign of tears and she had set forth a bottle of good wine. "Come in, do," she said. "Be seated. Let's discuss our situation." But when she poured the wine, she spilled some on the tablecloth.

"Has the captain examined the pictures we took?" Alexandra began.

Edith Poussin nodded. Her mouth grew tight. "Unquestionably that was a Kandemirian missile," she stated. "But one thing puzzles me. Those symbols written on the bulkhead near the pilot computer." As if to keep from looking at the pictures above her, she grabbed a sheet of paper. "Here, let me reproduce the lines. I won't copy them exactly. You'd have too much trouble distinguishing signs all of which are new to you. I'll substitute letters of our own alphabet. For this

wiggly thing in the middle of most of the lines,
I'll use a colon. Now see—" She wrote rapidly.

```
A B C D E F
M N O P Q MR
BA : PM
ABIJ : MOQMP
JEHC : NMQPPO
```

She continued similarly until everything had been
transferred, then threw her penstyl down. "There!
Can you make anything of that?"

"No," said Alexandra. "But weren't some of
those symbols actually Kandemirian numbers?"

"Yes. I've represented those by the letters A
through L. The others I've rendered as M through
R. I don't know what signs they are, what language or—Anyhow, you'll notice that they are
always separated from the Kandemirian numerals."

"I think," Sigrid ventured, "this must be a
conversion table."

"That's obvious, I would say," the captain
agreed. "But conversion into what? And why?"
She paused. "And who?"

Alexandra struck a fist on her knee. "Let us
not play games, Madame. The Kandemirian imperialists have subjugated many different language
groups on a dozen or more planets. This must
have been a notation made by some workman
belonging to an enslaved race."

"May have been," Edith Poussin corrected.
"We don't know. We dare not leap to conclu-

sions. Especially when we have been out of touch
with local events for more than two years."

Two years, Sigrid thought. Two magnificent
years. Not just the glory of the galaxy, new suns,
new folk, new knowledge as the *Europa* circum-
navigated the great Catherine's wheel of stars,
though that was enough splendour for a lifetime.
But the final proof to a continent still sceptical of
international cooperation and complete sexual
equality, that many nations together could do
this thing and that it could be done by women.

The years were bitter in her mouth.

She squared her shoulders. "What does Madame plan to do?" she asked.

The captain sipped for a while without answer.
"I am holding private conferences like this with
the most sensible officers," she admitted. "I am
open to suggestions."

"Let me, then, propose we go to . . . Monwaing,
or one of its colonies," Alexandra said. "We can
find out there what happened. And they will
help us."

Gertrud shuddered. "If they don't cut our
throats," she said. "Are you so sure they did not
do this? Yes, yes, those traders and teachers who
lived on Earth for years at a time, they were
polite and gentle, yes. But they were not human!"

"In any event," Edith Poussin said bleakly,
"no planet acts as a whole. The kindliest ordinary
citizens might have fiends for leaders." She
frowned at her wine. "I wish we had followed the
American and British example, and taken a non-
human pilot along, even though we were bound

for regions equally strange to everyone in this cluster. We might have got a little insight—No, I feel myself it is too risky to seek out anyone who might have had any interest, one way or another, in Earth's fate."

"What do we risk?" Alexandra murmured.

Sigrid raised her head. "There were other ships from Earth. They may still be out there."

"If the missiles haven't got them," Gertrud said. She snatched her glass and drank deeply.

"The all-male European expedition can't have got home," Sigrid declared. "They planned on at least three years in the Magellanic Clouds. No one knows where the Russians went, or the Chinese. And the Chinese crew included both sexes. And the Russians might have completed their own female ship and got her into space before— Maybe several other countries launched ships too. They were talking of it when we left. They were going to purchase ships, at least, now that they had the financial means." She clenched her jaw. "We'll meet someone again, someday."

"How?" Captain Poussin raised her brows. "The difficulties . . . well, I've threshed those out with the first and second mates already. There is no interstellar radio. If we go outside the local civilization-cluster, there is hardly any interstellar travel. How can two or three or a dozen dustmotes of ships, blundering blind in the galaxy, come upon each other before we die of old age?"

Sigrid stared at the deck, crossed and uncrossed her long legs, sent a warmth of wine down her

throat and listened to silence. There must be an
answer, she told herself desperately. Her father,
the shrewd and gentle ship's chandler who became a rich man by his own efforts, had taught
her to believe there was little men couldn't do if
they really wanted to. And women, he had added,
with his big laugh which she would not hear
again. When women set out to be an irresistible
force, he said, any immovable objects in the
neighbourhood had better get out of the way.

"We don't want to cower on some empty planet
where no one will ever come," Alexandra declared. "We should go to a civilization. Our skills
will be useful; we can earn our keep."

Sigrid nodded, recalling cities and ships where
folk had been mightily impressed. Not that humans were so outstanding in themselves, but
they carried the arts of their own cluster, which
were not identical with those of other places. A
blue-faced reptile had given her an energy gun in
exchange for one of her paintings; she had
delighted a six-limbed shipyard master by ex-
plaining to him certain refinements in the pilot
board which a British engineer had added to the
Monwaingi design. And this was in spite of their
having picked up only a few words of each other's
languages, in the brief time the *Europa* stayed.
Surely a hundred highly skilled Terrestrials could
make themselves valuable somewhere.

"To another civilization-cluster, then," Gertrud
said, almost eagerly. "That will be safest. No one
there will have any interest in . . . in hurting us.
We will come as total strangers."

"I believe so," the captain said. "You echo my own thoughts. However, the problem remains; if we go that far afield, how shall we inform any other surviving humans of our whereabouts? Of our existence, even?"

It was as if her father's laugh sounded in Sigrid's head. She sprang to her feet. Her glass tipped and crashed to the deck. No one noticed. "I have an idea, Madame!"

V

In this world a man must be either anvil or hammer.
—Longfellow

THE HALL WAS BUILT with massive dark timbers, the beam-ends chiselled into the gaping heads of sea monsters. Exquisitely carved screens from a former era emphasized rather than hid that brutal vigour which the single long room embodied. Fluorescent globes threw light off polished cups, shields, crowns, guns, booty from a dozen planets, and off the bronze wall plaques that displayed the emblems of Vorlak's warlords. At one end of the hall, flames roared and whirled up the chimney. The statue of the Overmaster at the other end was in shadow.

And that was symbolic, Donnan reflected. Eight thousand years of plantary unification had ended when the first space visitors came to Vorlak, two centuries ago. Now the imperium was a ghost, continuing its ghostly rituals in the High Palace at Aalstath. The reality of power was the Dragar class, masters of warships and warriors, touchy, greedy, recklessly brave—beings such as these, who sat their thrones down the length of the hall and stared over their golden goblets at the human.

Hlott Luurs, the Draga of Tolbek, leaned forward. The wooden serpents which trellised his seat cast gloom on the jewelled, many coloured lustre of his robes; but the muzzled, furry face was thrust plainly into the light. "Aye," he said, "as nearly as we know, Earth perished less than one of her own years agone. Otherwise the matter is a mystery."

The volume of his voice seemed to stir the battle banners hung from dimly seen rafters. Through open doors came a noise of surf and shrill night-birds; a saurian spouted and roared beyond the reef. The air filled Donnan's nostrils with cold unearthly smells.

He gauged his reply with care, according to what he knew about these folk. If he insulted them, he would be killed as soon as he left the sacred precincts of the council hall, and the orbiting *Franklin* would be blown to subatoms. On the other hand, a Draga was not insulted by the assumption he might be merciless.

"We came to Vorlak, my captain," he said, "because we did not really believe your people had done the deed. We thought to offer you our services in your war against Kandemir. But you will understand that first we've got to be certain you are not our enemy."

They both spoke in Uru, a modified form of the language used by the first interstellar visitors to this region. Some such *lingua franca* was necessary throughout a cluster; every spaceman mastered it as part of his training. Uru was flexible, grammatically streamlined, and included standardized units of measurement. Any oxygen breather could pronounce its phonemes, or at least write its alphabet, well enough to be understood. In fact, several other clusters, their own civilizations first seeded by explorers of that ancient race, had adopted the same auxiliary speech.

"You have my word we never harmed Earth," Hlott Luurs declared. "And I have been president of the Dragar Council for the past four years. I would have known."

He might not remain president, Donnan knew. The ever-shifting coalitions of these baronial admirals might overthrow him any day. But at the moment he dominated them, and therefore ruled his entire species.

To question his word of honour would be a mortal insult. And most likely he was telling the truth. Nevertheless—Donnan exchanged a glance with Ramri, whom he had taken along to this meeting. You'll know better how to be tactful, old chap, he appealed.

The shining blue Monwaingi form trod forward. "My captain, may I beg your indulgence?" Ramri fluted. "The situation among the Terrestrial crew is precarious. You can understand what shock the destruction of their planet was to them. Disorder culminated in near mutiny. Carl Donnan took the lead in restoring discipline, and was therefore elected chief. But as yet his authority is not firm. You must recall that modern humans have no tradition of absolute loyalty to one's captain. Many men questioned his decision to come here. Some are ignorant of Vorlakka customs. They would not realize that the word of Hlott Luurs is more than sufficient. Suspicious, they would cause trouble."

"Kill them," advised a Draga from the row of thrones.

"No," said Donnan harshly. "With almost the whole human race gone, I can't destroy any others for any reason."

"And yet," said Hlott, "you bring your ship here and offer to fight on our side."

"That's what we call a calculated risk." Donnan shifted on his feet. More and more, the situation began to look hopeless. They hadn't even given him a chair. That meant he was an inferior, a poor relation at best, fair game at worst.

His eyes flickered along the ranked captains. They were supposed to be humanoid, he reminded himself. Biped, about as tall as he was, with powerful arms ending in regular five-fingered hands, they were placental mammals and biochemically very similar to men. (That had been one reason for coming here. Humans could eat local food, which they could not on any Monwaingi planet.) But the torso was shorter and thicker, the legs longer and heavier, the feet webbed.

The head was flattened, low-browed, the brain case bulging out behind. The small external ears could fold to keep out water, the eyes had a nictitating membrane. The face was bluntly dog-like, black-nosed, with carnivore teeth. Sleek brown fur covered the entire body. This race was adapted to a planet whose land mass was mostly islands, which the tides of the nearby moon made into brackish swamps. Their history had eventuated in a maritime world empire, whose hereditary skippers and merchants had now—since the breakdown of the empire—become the Dragar, warlords and traders through an immense volume of space.

Silence waxed in the hall. It was broken by one who sat on Hlott's left. His plain black robe was conspicuous amidst that colour and metal. "Honourable Captain Donnan," he said, as softly as a Vorlakka throat could manage, "this unworthy person believes he has an indication that may serve as convincing evidence. Formerly it was a state secret, but the never-to-be-sufficiently-regretted destruction of your beautiful home has rendered such secrecy pointless. My captains know whereof I speak. If I may be allowed to use the archives?"

Stillness descended again. Even the fire and surf seemed to hush themselves. Odd, Donnan thought. Ger Nenna sat in this council as representative of the Overmaster, who was the merest figurehead. The imperial scholar-bureaucracy to which Ger belonged had even less reason for continued existence. And yet, grudgingly, the

Dragar deferred to him. Hlott rubbed a chinless jaw for two or three minutes, pondering. But in the end he said, "As the honourable minister will."

One refreshing aspect of feudalism was, to Donnan, the ease with which such decisions could be made. Ger Nenna rose, bowed, and walked across to a replicom unit. He stood punching buttons while the Dragar drank and servants hurried to refill their golden goblets. Ramri whispered in English: "Do you see any hope for our plans, Carl-my-friend?"

"Dunno," the man answered as softly.

"If we fail here—you will understand, will you not, how I can at once hope for your success and your failure?—surely then you will come to my home. I am positive we can offer still better proof of innocence than any which these beings possess."

Donnan tried to smile into the wistful beaked face. "You know *I* know you didn't do it," he said.

After getting the captaincy on Tau Ceti II, he had managed some change in Ramri's status. The avian was no longer in danger from the human crew. They accepted Donnan's making him unofficial first mate of the ship, though he was careful never to give any direct orders. There was no longer a guard on him. But if Donnan had sent Ramri home, the crew would not have liked it. They didn't accuse Monwaing of slaying Earth. They didn't know. The fact remained, however, that the Monwaingi planets had had the most to do with Earth and might thus most easily have found some reason to eliminate it. Until more facts were available, Ramri was a hostage of sorts. He accepted his status without complaint.

He reached quickly to give Donnan's arm a grateful squeeze. The replicom extruded a reel, duplicating material in the archives at Aalstath. Ger Nenna brought it over to Donnan.

"Naturally the honourable captain reads Russian," he said.

"A little," Donnan answered. "We got men aboard who're good at it."

"Then here is a treaty made between this Council and the Soviet Union, almost three years ago. The Russian exploratory ship which departed about the same time as your own, captain, carried officials empowered to deal with outworld governments. They concluded this agreement, which had been under secret negotiation for some time previously. The Soviet Union was to produce for us a large amount of arms in certain categories, at a favourable price; and numerous of their military personnel were to serve us as auxiliaries, thereby gaining experience in modern warfare. The Russian vessel then proceeded into far space, and we have no subsequent knowledge of it. But several armament cargoes were delivered to our ships—secretly, at a rendezvous on Venus. Here are copies of the manifests. And this correspondence shows that the first contingent of Soviet officers was due to depart for Vorlak very soon. Then the sorrow came that Earth was destroyed."

Donnan bent his attention to the reel. Yes, here were parallel Russian and Vorlakka texts.

He could read enough of the former to get the drift. "—common cause of the peace-loving peoples against imperialist aggressors . . . unity in the great patriotic struggle—" He didn't think any non-human could have done the phrasing that exactly. Plus all this other documentation. The Vorlakka would not have known the *Franklin* would arrive to ask for an accounting. They would hardly have prepared this file against an improbable contingency, the more so since they were openly contemptuous of the *Franklin's* power. Besides, the Dragar were not cloak-and-dagger types. If they had blown up Earth, they wouldn't have hidden the fact; not so elaborately, anyhow.

And the evidence fitted Terrestrial facts also. The Communists never had given up their ambitions, even when the fluid situation after the Monwaingi arrived forced them to pull in their horns while they reassessed matters. The secrecy of this agreement with Vorlak was not just to protect Earth against Kandemirian reprisal. It was so the Soviets could quietly get ahead of every other country in the development of a really up-to-date war machine. Here again, Donnan didn't believe that the Vorlakkar, who had never had any extensive contact with Earth, could have faked so precise a picture.

He was convinced.

He looked up. the lines from nose to mouth stretched and deepened in his face as he said: "Yes, my captains, proof aplenty. And further evidence against Kandemir. If their spies found out what was going on—" He couldn't continue.

"Quite likely," Hlott nodded. He seemed to have reached a decision while the human read. "Since you have come as our guests, begging sanctuary, and there is no feud between us, honour demands that we grant your wish. A place will be prepared for you. Your skills can earn you good pay in my own factories . . . unless, as I suspect, my honourable colleagues want a share of you. Return now to your boat, and see my chief aide tomorrow."

Donnan rallied his nerve. "Thanks, my captain," he said. "But we can't take that."

"What?" Hlott dropped a hand to the light axe at his waist. The Dragar leaned forward in their chairs. A hiss of indrawn breath went down their rank.

"We came as free people, freely offering our services," Donnan said. "We didn't come to be domesticated. Give us what we need and we'll fight for you. Otherwise, goodbye."

Hlott gnawed his lip. "You dare—" began a noble. Hlott shushed him and shrugged elaborately. "Goodbye," he said.

"My captain," Ger Nenna bowed low. "Unworthy, I pray your indulgence. Grant these folk their wish."

"Give them warships? Our painfully gathered intelligence of the enemy? These novices that never saw a space battle?" Hlott snorted an obscenity.

"My captain," said Ger, "these novices, as you call them, were not content to read texts and hear third-hand accounts of the galaxy. They set out for themselves. They have been to farther and stranger places than any Vorlakka skipper. They are no novices.

"Furthermore, their planet was in constant upheaval for nigh a century. My captain will recall that the Russians told us about guerrilla operations, border clashes, crafty international manoeuvrings. They understand war, these males who are your guests. They need only a little technical instruction. Thereafter . . . My captains hazard a ship or two. The Earthmen hazard not only their own lives, which of course are nothing, but conceivably the last life of their race. What Vorlakka would dare do likewise, with the spirits of his ancestors watching?"

Taken aback, Hlott said, "Well . . . even so—"

"A slime worm like myself may not remind my captains of their duty," Ger said. "And yet, does not the honour of a Draga require him to grant each person his own inalienable right? Food and protection to the groundling, justice and leadership to the crew member, respect to the colleague, deference to the Overmaster.

"These folk, who are freeborn, have come to be revenged on Kandemir, which murdered their planet—a murder so enormous that the hardest Draga must stand aghast. Vengeance is a right as well as a duty. Can the Dragar deny them their right?"

The fire roared on the hearth.

After a long while, Hlott nodded. "This is so. You shall have your right, Carl Donnan." With sudden, gusty good humour: "Who knows, you may deal Kandemir a strong blow. Bring him a chair, you scuts! Fill him a goblet. We'll drink to that!"

—Some time later, not altogether steady on his feet, Donnan left to return to his spaceboat. Ger Nenna accompanied him and Ramri. The hall's noise and brightness fell behind them as they walked downhill. The coppery shield of the moon, two degrees wide, was dropping swiftly horizonwards, but the island was still flooded by its light, icy, unreal, as if frost lay on the jungle behind and the beach in front, as if the docked submarines and seaplanes floated in a bath of mercury. Surf flamed white on the reef. The ocean churned and glowed beyond. Overhead the sky was strange. Nearly two hundred light-years from Earth, in the direction of Scorpio, the stars drew enigmatic pictures across the dark. Brightest among them, Antares burned blood red.

The wind, wet and pungent in his face, sobered Donnan. "I didn't have a chance to thank you before, Ger Nenna," he said. "Pardon me, but why did you help us? Your own class, the scholars, don't believe in revenge, do they?"

"No," said the black-robed one. "But we believe in justice. And . . . I think the galaxy has need of your race."

"Thanks," Donnan mumbled. He began to understand why the Overmaster's representatives were respected. Partly, to be sure, they symbolized the golden age, the Eternal Peace which Vorlak remembered so wistfully. But partly, too, they embodied wisdom. And the Dragar were at least wise enough collectively to feel the lack of wisdom in themselves.

"You jumped to conclusions, though," Donnan said. "I'm not entirely convinced Kandemir is guilty."

"Why, then, did you come here to fight against them, if I may presume to ask?"

"Well, we need employment, and I don't have any special compunctions about helping to stop them."

"You could have found safer employment, however, for your remnants. A factory job, such as was offered you."

"Yeah. Nice, humble obscurity." Donnan tamped his pipe, struck a light and fumed into the wind. "I don't believe we're the last survivors of our species. If we are, then our getting killed won't matter anyway; but I refuse to believe we are. I think a few other human ships must be scattered through the galaxy. If they haven't yet returned to the Solar System, they should be warned against doing so, or the missiles there may clobber them. If they have already come back, and escaped as we did, obviously they haven't gone to some planet in this cluster. We'd hear about that. So, they could be anywhere among a couple hundred billion stars. How can we get word to them?

"I figure one way is to make such a hooraw that the tale will go from end to end of the galaxy. There's some inter-cluster travel, after all. Not much, but some. Doubtless the news that a whole planet has been wiped out is already circulating. But over so much space and time and ignorance, people'll soon forget which one, or even where it is.

"What I'd like to do is produce a sensation they won't forget and won't garble too much. I don't know exactly what. Something about a footloose crew of bipeds who got their planet kicked out from under them and are raising the roof about it in this specific cluster. I hope that eventually the other human ships will hear the yarn and understand."

He laughed, a short metallic bark in the wind and moonlight. "A war is a good chance to make a splash," he finished. "And here we got a war ready-made."

VI

Hell from beneath is moved for thee to meet thee at thy coming.

—*Isaiah, xiv, 9*

THE HOT F6 DWARF that was Kandemir's sun lay about 175 light-years from Vorlak, northwards and clockwise. Although its third planet was somewhat heavier than Earth, the intense irradiation had thinned and dried the atmosphere. Even so, a man who took precautions against ultra-violet could live on Kandemir and eat most of the food.

History there had taken an unusual course. Vast fertile plains fostered the growth on one continent of a nomadic society which conquered the sedentary peoples. This was not like cases on Earth when barbaric wanderers overran a civilization. On Kandemir, the nomads were the higher culture, those who invented animal domestication, writing, super-tribal government, and machine technology. The cities became mere appendages where helots laboured at the tasks such as mining which could not move with the seasons. When the nomads learned how to cross Kandemir's small shallow oceans, their way of life soon dominated the world. Warfare and economic competition between their hordes spurred the advent of an industrial revolution. But gunpowder, steam engines, and mass production shifted the balance. Nomad society could not readily assimilate them; it developed strains. A century ago, Kandemir had become as chaotic as the last years of Earth. Then explorers from T'sjuda came upon it and began to trade.

Numerous Kandemirians went to space as students, workers, and mercenary soldiers—for T'sjuda, like Xo and some other powers, was not above occasional imperialism on backward planets. The Kandemirians returned home with new ideas for revitalizing their old culture. Under Ashchiza the Great, the Erzhuat Horde forced unification on Kandemir and launched a feverish programme of modernization; but one adapted to nomadism. The cybernetic machine replaced the helot, the spaceship replaced the wagon, the clans became the crews of distinct fleets. Soon Kandemirian merchants and adventurers swarmed through space. Yet their tradition bound them to the mother world, where they returned for those seasonal rites of kinship that corresponded in them to a religion. Thus the Grand Lord remained able to command their allegiance.

As time passed, their habits (which others interpreted as cruelty, arrogance, and greed) brought them ever more often into conflict with primitive races. These were easy prey. But this, increasingly, caused trouble with advanced worlds such as T'sjuda, who had staked out claims of their own. Action and reaction spiralled into open battle on the space frontiers. Defeated at first, Kandemir rallied so violently that its enemies asked for terms. The peace settlement was harsh; in effect, the one-time teachers of the nomads became their vassals.

The little empire which thus more or less happened in the time of Ashchiza's son began to grow more rapidly under his grandson Ferzhakan. Decentralized and flexible, nomadic overlordship was well suited to the needs of interstellar government; the empire worked. For glory, wealth, and protection—most especially to gain the elbow room which Kandemirian civilization required in ever greater quantities, for space traffic as well as for the gigantic planetary estates of its chieftains—the empire must expand. Ferzhakan dreamed of ultimate hegemony over this entire spiral arm.

His policy soon brought an opposing coalition into existence. This was dominated by the Vorlakka Dragar, who also had far-flung interests. The nomad fleet was stopped at the Battle of Gresh. But that fight was a draw. Neither side could make further headway. The war settled down to years of raids, advances and retreats, flareups and stalemates, throughout the space between the two planets. Well off to one side, Monwaing and her daughters maintained what was officially an armed neutrality, in practice an assistance and encouragement of Vorlak. The other independent, space-travelling races in the cluster were too weak to make much difference.

The nearest strong Kandemirian base to Vorlak was forty light-years off, at a star the Vorlakkar called Mayast. As his borrowed destroyer slipped from the last interference fringe and accelerated inwards on paragrav, Donnan saw it burn blue-white in the forward viewscreen. Like a fire balloon to starboard, the biggest planet of the system glowed among specks that were moons. Howard, now chief navigator, swung his scopes and poised fingers over the calculator keyboard. "No," said Ramri. "the declination is eleven point four two degrees—" He broke off. "You are right. I was wrong. Forgive me."

Even in that moment, Donnan grinned. Despite his wide experience, Ramri could still get number systems confused. It was more than the different planets using different symbols; the mathematics varied intrinsically. The Monwaingi based their arithmetic on six. But this was a Vorlakka ship, whose ten-fingered builders used a decimal system like Earth's.

Howard ignored the avian, but Olak Faarer, the Draga observer, scowled and recomputed the fix for himself. He made no bones about doubting the competence of the fifty Terrestrials who had taken over the *Hrunna*. They had demonstrated their skill after a month of lessons, as well as on the days of their voyage hither. But the Vorlakka aristocrat remained scornful of them.

As far as that goes, Donnan reflected, the rest of the boys, waiting back on the *Franklin* in orbit around Vorlak, didn't look any too confident in us. Does seem like a hare-brained stunt at that. One lone destroyer, to punch through these defences, approach so close to the enemy base that they can't stop our missile barrage, and then get away unsinged! When the Vorlakkar have been trying for a decade. . . .

He looked at Goldspring. "Anything registered yet?" he asked. Foolish question, he realized at once. He'd be told the moment that haywired instrument over which the physicist was crouched gave a wiggle. But damn it, you could talk as big as you pleased: when you sailed to battle your heart still banged and you wanted a beer in the worst way. Silliness was excusable.

"N-no. I'm not sure. Wait. Wait a minute."

In one minute, forty gravities' acceleration, the *Hrunna* added better than fourteen miles per second to an already tremendous velocity. Goldspring nodded. "Yes. Two moving sources over in that direction." He read off the co-ordinates. Donnan tapped a few pilot keys, spinning the ship about and applying full thrust orthogonally to her path. After three or four minutes, Goldspring nodded "Okay," he said. "We're beyond range."

Howard studied the integrated data on his meters and punched out a new set of vectors in the control board. The ship had never actually departed from her sunward plunge—so high a velocity was not soon killed—but she began a modification of path, correcting for the previous force, so as to rendezvous with Mayast II according to plan.

Olak Faarer glided across the bridge and gazed at the steady oscilloscope trace on Goldspring's instrument. "What were they, those objects you detected?" he asked. "Ships, unmanned patrol missiles, or what?"

"I don't know," Goldspring said. "My gizmo isn't that good . . . yet. I only know they were sources of modulated paragravitic force, at such-and-such a distance, velocity, and acceleration. In other words, they were something running under power." He added dryly, "We may assume that anything under power in this system is dangerous."

"So is anything in free fall," Olak grumbled.

"Oh, Lord," Donnan groaned. "How often must I tell you—um-m-m—that is, surely my honourable colleague understands that, at such speed as we've got, nothing which doesn't have a velocity comparable in both magnitude and direction is likely to be able to do much about us."

"Yes, yes," Olak said stiffly. "I have had your device explained to me often enough. A paragrav detector with unprecedented sensitivity. I admit it is a good instrument."

"Only the first of a long series of instruments," Goldspring promised. "And weapons. My staff and I have barely begun to explore the possibilities opened by our new theory of space-time-energy relationships. The workers on the *Franklin* may already have a surprise for us when we get home."

"Perhaps," Olak said with impatience. "Nonetheless, I did not say anything hitherto, lest I be thought a coward. But now that we are irrevocably committed, I tell you frankly that this trusting our lives to a single hand-made prototype of a single minor invention is utter foolishness."

Donnan sighed. "I've argued this out a thousand times with a hundred Dragar," he said. "I thought you were listening. Okay, then, I'll explain again.

"Arn's gadget there doesn't merely respond to paragrav waves like the ordinary detector. It generates microwaves of its own, and thus it can use interferometric principles. The result is, it can spot other ships twice as far and three times as accurately as the best conventional instrument.

"Well, if we're aware of the enemy long before they can detect us, we can take evasive action and stay beyond their own instrumental range. Your previous raids have failed because the system is so thick with patrol ships and orbital missiles. Your squadrons were homed on before they got near the base planet. But by the time we today get so close they can't help spotting us, we'll also be travelling too fast to intercept. So will the torps we launch. We'll zip right through their inner defences, wipe out their fort, and reach the opposite interference fringe before they've had time to sneeze."

Olak had bristled with increasing indignation as Donnan's insulting résumé of what everyone knew proceeded. The Draga flashed teeth. "I am not a cub, colleague," he growled. "I have heard this many times before."

"Then may I beg my honoured colleague to act as if he had?" Donnan murmured.

Olak clapped a hand to his sidearm. Donnan locked eyes with him. After a few seconds that quivered, the Draga gave way. He stamped over to the port screen and glared out at the stars.

Donnan permitted himself a moment of untensing. That had been a near thing. These otter-faced samurai had tempers like mercury fulminate. But he had to get the moral jump on them. Eventually they must become *his* allies—or the tale of the last Earthmen would not be colourful enough to cross the galaxy. And the best means of putting them down, however dangerous, seemed to be to outpride them.

"Hold it!" Goldspring rattled off a series of figures. Donnan and Howard modified course again.

"That one's up ahead, right?" Donnan asked.

"Yes," Goldspring tugged his beard. "May have been looking for us."

"I thought I picked up a trace a few minutes ago," said Wells at the radar. "I didn't mention it, because it was gone right away. Could have been an automatic spy station . . . which could have alerted yonder ship."

Donnan nodded. Everybody had realized nothing could be done about that. Black-painted, solar-powered, of negligible mass, a detector station in orbit could not be avoided by the *Hrunna*. Any ship which passed close would be spotted by its instruments and a warning would be beamcast to the nearest patrol units. Spaceships would then go looking for the stranger. However, Donnan expected to detect those searchers in ample time to elude their own instruments.

Still, he wished a station had not blabbed so early in the game. Perhaps the Kandemirians were even more thorough about their defences than Vorlakka intelligence had indicated.

He got out his pipe and reached for his pouch. But no. Better not. Almost out of tobacco. Ration yourself, son, till you can locate a substitute somewhere. . . . The thought led him to wine, and horses, and Alison, and every beloved thing that would not exist again. He chewed savagely on the cold pipe.

The destroyer flung herself onwards. Men swapped a few words, attempted jokes, shifted at their posts and stared at their weapons. On the gun deck Yule, whom Donnan had pardoned for the murder of Bowman but whom no one quite trusted any longer, huddled against his torpedo tube as if the launching coils were his mother. Up on the bridge, Ramri and the standby navigator played chess. Slowly the blue sun swelled in the screens. Ever more often, the ship moved crab-wise to evade being detected.

Until:

"That vessel registering now is running very nearly parallel to us, at about the same speed and acceleration," Goldspring computed. "We'll enter the effective range of his instruments before long."

"Can't avoid him, eh?" Donnan said.

"No. The enemy craft have got too thick. See, if we dodge this way we'll run smack into this cluster of boats"—Goldspring pointed to a chart he was maintaining—"and if we deviate very far in the other direction, we'll be spied by that large craft yonder. And he could loose quite a barrage, I'm sure. We'll do our best to hold our present vector and take our chances with the ship I just mentioned."

"Hm, I dunno. If his own vectors are so similar to ours—"

"Not similar enough. He'd have to accelerate at thirty gees to get really near us. And he's a cruiser, at least, judging from the power of his emission. A cruiser can't do thirty."

"A cruiser's torpedoes can do a hundred or more."

"I know. He probably will fire at us. But according to my data, with our improved detection capability, we'll have sighting information at least ten seconds in advance of his. So our broadside will intercept his completely—nothing will get through—at a distance of half a kilomile."

"Well," Donnan sighed, "I'll take your word for it. This was bound to happen sooner or later."

Olak's eyes filmed and his nostrils flared. "I

had begun to fear we would see no combat on this mission," he said.

"That would'a suited me fine," Donnan answered. "Space war's too hard on my nerves. A bare-knuckled brawl is kinda fun, but this sitting and watching while a bunch of robots do your fighting for you feels too damned helpless. . . . Steady as she goes, then."

They weren't very far from the planet, he told himself. In another hour they could discharge their missiles. But that hour might get a bit rough.

Gunnery was out of his department. His officers' orders barked in his awareness, but he paid little attention. Hands loose on the pilot board, he thought mostly about Earth. There had been a girl once, not Alison, though Alison's lips had also been sweet. . . . Sparks flared and died among the stars. "One, two, three, four," Goldspring counted. "Five, six!"

"No more?" Ramri asked from the chessboard.

"No. Nothing more registers. We intercepted his whole barrage. And we've three torps left over that are still moving. They just might zero in on that fellow."

"Excellent," said Ramri. He tapped the sweating man who sat across the board from him. "Your move, Lieutenant . . . Lieutenant! Do you feel all right?"

Wells yelled. Donnan didn't stop to look. He crammed on a full sideways vector. Engines roared. Too late! For a bare instant, the sternward screen showed him the heavy, clumsy object that darted from low larboard. Then the deck rolled beneath him. He saw it split open. A broken girder drove upwards and sheared the head off Ramri's chess partner.

Blood geysered. The crash of explosion struck like a fist in the skull. Donnan was hurled against his safety web. Olak Faarer, who had not been seated, cart-wheeled past him, smashed into the panel and bounced back, grotesquely flopping. Paragrav was gone; weightlessness became an endless tumble, through smoke and screams, thunderous echoes, the hiss of escaping atmosphere. Blood drops danced in the air, impossibly red.

The screens went blank. The lights went out. Too weak to be felt as such, the pseudogravity of the ship's lunatic spin sent wreckage crawling within the smashed hull. End over end, the ruin whirled on a hyperbolic orbit towards the blue sun.

VII

Then endure for a while, and live for a happier day
—Virgil

PRISONER!

He had been one twice before, on a vag rap in some Arkansas tank town and then, years afterwards, when a bunch of Chinese "volunteers" overran the Burmese valley where he was building a dam. But Donnan didn't care to think about either occasion, now. At their worst, those jails had stood on a green and peopled Earth.

The sky overhead was like incandescent brass. He couldn't look near the sun. Squinting against its lightning-coloured glare, he saw the horizon waver with mirage. A furnace wind sucked moisture from skin and nose: he heard its monotonous roar as background to the crunch of boot-soles on gravel. And yet this was not a desert. Clusters of serpentine branches with leathery brown fingers rose thickly on every side, tossing and snapping in the blast. Overhead glided a kite-shaped animal whose skin glittered as if strewn with mica. The same glint was on the scales of the natives, who otherwise looked more like giant four-legged spiders with quadruple eyes and tentacular arms than anything else. No doubt they found this environment pleasant, as did the Kandemirian platoon to whom they kowtowed.

Donnan had rarely felt so alone. Failure, the death of ten men who trusted him and the captivity of forty others, had been horrible in him since the moment the enemy frigate laid alongside and the boarding party entered. There wasn't much the humans could have done except surrender, of course. Their ship was a hulk, only spacesuits kept them alive, few even had a sidearm. They shambled to the other craft and waited apathetically in irons while they were ferried to Mayast II.

And now some big cheese wants to interrogate me himself, Donnan thought dully. How can I breathe the same air as Earth's murderers?

The beehive native huts which straggled around the fortifications were left behind as the platoon passed a steel gate and entered a mountainous concrete dome. The warren inside was unimportant, Donnan knew, frosting on the cake. The real base was buried deep in the planet's crust. Even so, his barrage could have wrecked it; if—

Activity hummed around him, tall Kandemirian

forms striding with tools and weapons and papers down rubbery-floored corridors, offices where they squatted before legless desks under the arching leaves of uzhurun plants. They did not speak unnecessarily. The stillness was uncanny after the booming wind outside. The odour overwhelmed him, acrid and animal.

He must concede they were handsome. A seven-foot humanoid with exaggerated breadth of shoulders and slenderness of waist looks idealized rather than grotesque. So did the nearly perfect ovoid of the head, its curve hardly broken by wide greenish-blue eyes with slit pupils, tiny nose, the peculiarly human and sensitive lips. Behind the large, pointed ears, a great ruff of hair framed the face. Otherwise the skin was glabrous, silken smooth; the mobile twin tendrils on the upper lip were scent organs. The hands were also humanoid, in spite of having six fingers and jet-black nails. The dignified appearance was enhanced by austere form-fitting clothes in subdued colours. Against this, the blazons of rank and birth stood startlingly forth.

Donnan felt dumpy in their presence. He straightened his shoulders. So what, by God!

A door, above which was painted a giant eye, flew open. The guard platoon halted, not stiffly and with clattering heels as Earth's soldiers had been wont, but gliding to a partial crouch. Each touched to his head the stubby barrel of his cyclic rifle. Someone whistled within. The leader nudged Donnan forward. The door closed again behind the man.

One guard stood in a corner, watchful. Otherwise the room's only occupant was a middle-aged officer whose clan badge carried the pentacle of supreme nobility. He belonged to that Kandemirian race whose skin was pale gold and whose ruff was red. A scar seamed one cheek. Still squatting, he smiled up at Donnan. "Greeting, shipmaster," he said in fluent Uru. "I bid you welcome." He arched naked brows with a most human sardonicism. "If you choose to accept my sentiments."

Donnan nodded curtly and lowered himself tailor fashion to the floor. The Kandemirian touched a button on his desk. "You see Tarkamat of Askunzhol, who speaks for the Baikush Clan and for the field command of the Grand Fleet," he said without pretentiousness.

Almost, Donnan himself whistled. The high admiral in person, director of combat operations along the whole Vorlakka front! "I had no idea . . . we'd be of this much interest," he managed to say. "Uh—"

A silver plate in the desktop slid back and a tray emerged with two cups of some hot liquid. "What records about your species I could find in the files of this base," Tarkamat said, "mention that indak will not hurt you. In fact, many of you find—found the beverage pleasant."

Automatically, Donnan reached for a cup! *No!* He yanked his hand back as if it had been scalded.

Tarkamat made a purring noise that might correspond to laughter. "Believe me, if I wished you drugged, I would order that done. What I offer you with the indak is the status of . . . no, not quite a guest, but more than a captive. Drink."

Donnan began to shake. He needed a while before he could stammer, "I, I, I'll be damned if I'll take anything . . . from you! From any murdering sneak . . . of a Kandemirian."

The soldier tilted his rifle and growled. Tarkamat hushed him with a soft trill. For a moment the admiral studied his prisoner, scarred countenance enigmatic. Then, very quietly, he said: "Do you believe my folk annihilated yours? But you are wrong. We had no part in that deed."

"Who did, then?" Donnan shouted. He started to rise, fists knotted, but sank down again and struggled for breath.

The red-ruffed head wove back and forth. "I do not know, shipmaster. Our intelligence service has made some effort to learn who is responsible, but thus far has failed. Vorlak seems the likeliest possibility."

"No." Donnan gulped towards a degree of self-possession. "I was there. They showed me proof they were innocent."

"What proof?"

"A treaty—" Donnan stopped.

"Ah, so. Between themselves and some Terrestrial nation? Yes, we knew about that, from various sources." Tarkamat made a negligent gesture. "We feel quite sure that none of the minor independent powers, such as Xo, struck at Earth. They lack both resources and motive."

"Who's left but Kandemir, then?" Donnan's voice was jagged and strange in his own ears.

"Earth—one nation of Earth, at least— was helping your enemies; that's motive. And the Solar System is patrolled by your robot missiles. I took photographs."

"So did we," Tarkamat answered imperturbably. "We sent an expedition there to look about when we heard the news. It, also, was attacked. But the Mark IV Quester is, frankly, not the best weapon of its type. Hundreds have been captured by foreign powers, enemy and neutral, through being disabled or having their computers jammed or simply because their warheads were duds. Someone who wished to blacken our name—and has, in fact, succeeded, because few people believe our denials—such a party could have accumulated those missiles for the purpose. Please note, too, that the Mark IV is not ordinarily as slow and awkward as those encountered in the Solar System. Does that not suggest they were deliberately throttled down to make sure that there would be escapers to carry the tale?"

"Or to give your propaganda exactly the argument you've just given me," Donnan growled. "You can't sweep under the rug that the treaty between Russia and Vorlak gave you reason to destroy Earth."

"Then why have we not made a similar attempt on Monwaing?" Tarkamat countered. "They, in their alleged neutrality, have been more useful to the Vorlakka cause for a much longer time than one country on Earth supplying a few shiploads of small arms." He lifted his head, superciliously. "We have refrained, not from squeamishness, but because the effort would be out of proportion to the result. Especially since a living planet is far more valuable to us in the long run. We could not colonize a Monwaingi world without sterilizing it first; but, despite the cooler sun, we could have planted ourselves firmly on Earth . . . if we chose . . . when we got around to it. The bio-chemistries are enough alike."

His tone hardened: "Do not imagine your world, or any country on it, amounted to anything militarily. Had that one nation, the Ro-si-ya or whatever it was called, had it proven a serious annoyance, do you know what we would have done? If simple threats would not make them desist, we would have used the tried and true process which has gained Kandemir easy domination over five other backward planets. We would have sent a mission to the Terrestrial rivals of Ro-si-ya, pointed out how strong she was becoming in relation to them, and made them our cat's paws. Why expend good Kandemirian lives to conquer Earth when the Earthlings themselves would have done half the work for us?"

Donnan bit his lip. He hated to admit how the argument struck home. What he remembered of human history told him how often a foreign invader had entered as the ally of one local faction. Romans in Greece, Saxons in Britain, English in Ireland and India, Spaniards in Mexico—*If I forget thee, O Jerusalem!*

"Very clever," he said. "Have you any actual proof?"

Tarkamat smiled. "Who is interrogating whom,

shipmaster? Accept my word or not, as you choose. Frankly, the clans care little what others think of them. However," he added more seriously, "we are not fiends. Look about you with unprejudiced eyes. Our overlordship may seem harsh at times. And it is in fact, when our interests so require. But our proconsuls are not meddlesome. They respect ancient usage. The subject peoples gain protection and share in the prosperity of an ever-widening free trade sphere. We do not drain their wealth. If anything, they live better than the average Kandemirian."

Harking back over what he had learned, Donnan must needs nod. The Spartan virtues of the nomads did include governmental honesty. "You forget one thing," he said. "They aren't free any longer."

"So your culture would claim," Tarkamat replied with sudden brutality. "But your culture is dead. What use can sentimentality be to you? Make the best of your situation."

"I'm sentimental enough not to collaborate with whoever killed my people," Donnan snapped.

"I told you Kandemir did not. Your opinion is of insufficient importance to me for me to belabour that subject further. A handful of rootless mercenaries like yourselves hardly seem worth keeping prisoner even. Except . . . for the astonishingly deep penetration you made of our defences. I want to know how that was done."

"Luck. You got us in the end, after all."

"By using a new device we had been reserving for the next major battle."

"I can guess what that was," Donnan said, hoping to postpone the real unpleasantness. (Why? he wondered. What did it matter? What did anything matter?) "Missiles, like ships, operate on paragrav these days, to get the range and acceleration that it offers. So counter-missiles are equipped with paragrav detectors. They home on the engines of a target object. Only if the engine is switched off do they use radar, infra-red, and other shorter-range equipment. Well, you used a big paragrav job to match vectors with our ship. We spotted it easily. But it didn't try to zero on us. It ran parallel instead, and released a flight— not of regular torps, but of rockets. We weren't on the lookout for anything so outmoded. Over that short distance, an atomic-powered ion drive could rendezvous with us. We didn't know it was there till it was too late to dodge."

"Actually, you were hit by only one rocket out of several," Tarkamat confessed. "But one suffices. You would have been been blown to gas, had our anxiety to know your secret not made us pre-set the warheads for minimal blast."

"There is no secret." Donnan felt sweat gather in his armpits and trickle down his ribs. Before him wavered the image of Goldspring, half stunned, bleeding in the face, elbowing aside the wreckage and the dead that bobbed around him, by flashbeam light ripping and hammering the detector into shapelessness while the enemy frigate closed in.

"There most certainly is," Tarkamat stated flatly. "Statistical analysis of what course data we have for you strongly suggests you were able to detect us at unprecedented distances. Our own best paragrav instruments are crowding the theoretical limit of sensitivity. Therefore you employed some new principle. This in turn may conceivably lead to entire new classes of weapons. I do not intend to play games, shipmaster. I presume you have no great emotional attachment to Vorlak, but some to your crew. One crewman per day will be executed before your eyes until you agree to collaborate. The method of execution I have in mind takes several hours."

I expected something like this, Donnan thought. Coldness and greyness drowned his spirit. As if from immensely far away, he heard Tarkamat continue:

"If you co-operate, you can expect good treatment. You will be settled on a congenial planet. Any other humans who may be found can join you there. An able species like yours can surely fit itself into the framework set by the imperium. But I warn you against treachery. You will be allowed to build and demonstrate your devices, but under the close supervision of our own physicists, to whom the principles involved must be explained beforehand. Since I presume you left people behind at Vorlak, who will also be working along these lines, delays shall not be tolerated. Very well, shipmaster, give me your answer."

Why keep on? the mind sighed in Donnan. Why not surrender? Maybe they really did not bomb Earth. Maybe the best thing is to become their serfs. Oh, Jesus, but I'm tired.

I was tired in that Burma prison camp too, he thought drearily. I didn't believe we'd ever get sprung, me and the others. Barbed wire, jungle, sloppy-looking guards with almighty quick guns, miserable villagers who didn't dare help us—But that was on Earth. There was still a future then. We could plan on . . . on sunrise, and moonrise, and rain and wind and light; on the game continuing after we ourselves stopped playing. So, we didn't stop. We cooked up a hundred plans for crashing out. One of 'em, at least, was pretty good. Might have worked, if the diplomats hadn't arranged our release about that time. If it had not worked, well, we'd have been decently dead, shovelled down into an earth that still lived.

That's why I've gone so gutless, he thought. Now there's nothing in space or time except my own piddling self.

The hell there isn't!

The knowledge burst within him. He sat straight with an oath.

Tarkamat regarded him over a steaming cup. "Well, shipmaster?" he murmured.

"We'll do what you want," Donnan said. "Of course."

VIII

Mit shout and crash and sabre flash.
And vild husaren shout
De Dootchmen boorst de keller in,
Und rolled de lager out;
Und in the coorlin' powder shmoke,
Vhile shtill de pullets sung,
Dere shtood der Breitmann, axe in hand,
A knockin' out de boong.
    Gling, glang, gloria!
    Victoria! Encoria!
De shpicket beats de boong.

—Leland

FROM THEIR WINDOW high in that tower known as i-Chula—the Clouded—Sigrid Holmen and Alexandra Vukovic could easily see aro-Kito, One Who Awaits. That spire lifted shimmering walls and

patinaed bronze roof above most of its neighbours; otherwise its corkscrew ramps and twisted
buttresses were typical Eyzka architecture. The
operations within, however, resembled none which
had yet been seen on Zatlokopa, or in this entire
civilization-cluster. Terran Traders, Inc., had
leased the whole building.

As yet the company was not big enough to fill
every room. There was no reason why the *Europa*
crew should not live there, and a number of the
women did. But some, like Sigrid and Alexandra,
had to get away from their work physically or
explode. They took lodgings throughout the city.

Occasionally, though, as the company's growth
continued, work sought them out. This evening
Alexandra was bringing an important potential
client home for dinner. The sha-Eyzka were very
human in that respect; they settled more deals
over dessert and liqueurs than over desks and
distocribes. If Terran Traders could please Taltla
of the sha-Oktzu, and land that house's account,
a big step forward would have been taken.

Sigrid looked at her watch. By now she was
used to the time units, eight-based number system, and revolving clock faces employed here.
Damn! The others would arrive in ten minutes,
and she hadn't perfumed yet.

A moment she lingered, savouring the fresh air
that blew across her skin. Zatlokopa was not only
terrestroid, but midway through an interglacial
period, climatically a paradise for humans. The
women had quickly adopted a version of native
dress, little more than shorts and sandals, with

the former only for the sake of pockets. The sun slanted long rays across the towers, a goldenness that seemed to fill the atmosphere. How quiet it was!

Too quiet, she thought. A winged snake cruised above the many-steepled skyline, but nothing else moved, no ground-cars, no fliers, not a walker in the grassy lanes between buildings or a boat on the sunset-yellow canals. The city had subways, elevated tunnel-streets that looped like vines from tower to tower, halls and shaftways in the houses themselves. This was not Earth, she knew, it never had been, never could be. Nothing could ever again be Earth.

A spaceship lifted silent on paragravity, kilometres distant and yet so big that she saw sunlight burn along its flanks. The Holdar liner, she thought; we have a consignment aboard. That reminded her. She had no time for self-pity. Closing the window, she hurried into the kitchen and checked the auto-chef. Everything seemed under control. Thank God for the high development of robotics in this cluster. No human cook had the sense of taste and smell to prepare a meal that an Eyzka would think fit to eat.

Sigrid returned to the living room, where Earthtype furniture looked homely and lost amidst intricate vaulting and miniature fountains. The perfume-cabinet slid open for her. She consulted a chart. Formality on Zatlokopa paid no attention to clothes, but made a ritual of odours. For entertaining a guest of Taltla's rank, you used a blend of Class Five aerosols. . . . She wrinkled her nose. Everything in Class Five smelled alike to her—rather like ripe silage. Well, she could drench herself with . . . let's see, the sha-Eyzka usually enjoyed cologne, and there was some left from the ship. . . . Her hand closed on the little cut-glass bottle.

The door said: "Two desire admittance."

Had Alexandra brought the fellow here early? She'd been *told* not to. "Let them in," Sigrid said without looking at the scanner. The door opened.

Blank metal met her eyes. Not sun-browned human skin or the green and gold fur of an Eyzka, but polished alloy. The robots were approximately humanoid, a sheer two and a half metres tall. She stared up, and up, to faceless heads and photoelectric slits. Those glowed dull red, as if furnaces burned behind.

"*Kors i Herrans namn!*" she exclaimed. "What's this?"

One glided past her, cat-silent. The other extended an arm and closed metal fingers on her shoulder, not hard, but chilling. She tried indignantly to step back. The grip tightened. She sucked in a gasp.

The other robot came back. It must have checked if she was alone. The first said: "Come. You need not be harmed, but make no trouble." It spoke Uru, which was also the interstellar auxiliary language in this cluster as in several others.

"What the blazes do you mean?" Anger drove out fear.

Hearing her speak in Eyzka, the robot shifted

to that language, fluent though accented. It laid its free hand on her head. The fingers nearly encircled her skull. "Come, before I squeeze," it ordered.

That grip could crush her temples like an almond shell. "Make no outcry," the second robot warned. Its accent was even thicker.

Numbly, she accompanied them out. The corridor was a tube from nowhere to nowhere; doors were locked and blind; only the ventilators, gusting a vegetable smell in her face, made any noise. Her skin turned cold and wet, her lips tingled. They picked the right hour for kidnapping, she thought in hollowness. Nearly everyone is still at work, or else inside preparing for the workers' return. You won't find casuals moving about, as you would in a human city. This is not Earth. Earth is a cinder, ten thousand light-years distant.

She grew aware of a pain in one hand. With a dull astonishment, she saw that she still gripped the cologne bottle. The faceted glass had gouged red marks into her palm.

Suddenly she lifted the thing, unscrewed the atomizer nose and poured the contents over her head.

Steel fingers snatched it from her. They took a good deal of skin along too. Sigrid tried not to whimper with pain. She sucked her hand while the twin giants bent their incandescent gaze on the bottle. The throbbing eased. No bones seemed broken. . . .

The robots conferred in a language she didn't

know. Then to her, in sharp Eyzka: "Attempted suicide?"

"The liquid isn't corrosive," the other machine observed.

You noseless idiot! Sigrid thought wildly. She jammed her bleeding hand into one pocket and let them hustle her along.

Footfalls were inaudible. Nothing lived, nothing stirred, save themselves. They went down a dropshaft to a tunnel. A public gravsled halted at an arm signal. They boarded and it accelerated smoothly along its route.

They aren't independent robots, Sigrid decided. She was becoming able to think more coolly now. *They're remote-control mechanisms. I've never seen their type before. But then, there are thousands of kinds of automaton in this galactic region, and I've been here less than a year. Yes, they're just body-waldos.*

But whose? Why?

Not natives. The sha-Eyzka had received the humans kindly, in their fashion: given them the freedom of Zatlokopa, taught them language and customs, heard their story. After that the newcomers were on their own, in the raw capitalism which dominated this whole cluster. But a small syndicate of native investors had been willing to take a flyer and help them get started. There wasn't much question of commercial rivalry yet. The women's operations were too radically unlike anything seen before. Carriers and brokers existed in plenty throughout this cluster, but not on the scale which Terran Traders contemplated—

nor with such razzle-dazzle innovations as profit sharing, systems analysis, and motivational research among outworld cultures. So the kidnappers were not likely to be Eyzka competitors.

The accent with which the robots spoke, and the failure of their operators to guess what was in the cologne bottle, also suggested—

The sled halted for a native passenger. He bounded on gracefully, beautiful as a hawk or a salmon had been beautiful on Earth. Steel fingers clenched about Sigrid's wrist till she felt her bones creak. She didn't cry out, though. "Not one sign to him," the robot murmured in Uru.

"If you let me go, I won't," she managed.

The pressure slackened. She leaned weakly back on the bench. The Eyzka gave her a startled glance, took out a perfumed handkerchief, and moved pointedly as far from her as he could.

Presently she was taken off the sled. Down another ramp, through another passage, twist, turn, a last downwards spiral, a dark dingy tunnel with a hundred identical doors, and one that opened for her. She stepped through between the robots. The door closed again at her back.

A dozen creatures sat at a table. They were squat and leathery, with flat countenances. Two more were at a waldo panel in the rear of the room. Those had obviously been guiding the robots. They also turned to face her, and the machines flanking Sigrid became statues. The room was redly lit, shadowy and cold. A record player emitted a continuous thin wailing.

Forsi, Sigrid realized. The second most power-ful race in this cluster. She might have guessed.

One goblin leaned towards her. His skin rus-tled as he moved. "There is no reason to waste time," he clipped. "We have already learned that you stand high among the sha-Terra. The highest ranking one, in fact, whom it was practicable for us to capture. You will co-operate or suffer the consequences. Understand, to Forsi commercial operations are not merely for private gain, as here on Zatlokopa, but are part of a larger de-sign. You, Terran Traders' Corporation, have upset the economic balance of this cluster. We extrapo-late that the upsetting will grow exponentially if not checked. In order to counteract your opera-tions, we must have detailed information about their rationale and the fundamental psychology behind it. You have shrewdly exploited the fact that no two species think entirely alike and that you yourselves, coming from an altogether foreign civilization-complex, are doubly unpredictable. We shall take you home with us and make studies."

Despite herself, Sigrid's knees wobbled. She struggled not to faint.

"If you co-operate fully, the research may not damage you too much," said the Forsi. "At least, the work will not be made unnecessarily painful. We bear you no ill will. Indeed, we admire your enterprise and only wish you had chosen our planet instead of Zatlokopa." He shrugged. "But I daresay climate influenced you."

"And society." Despite herself, her voice was husky with fear. "A decent culture to live in."

He was not insulted. Another asked curiously, "Did you search long before picking this culture?"

"We were lucky," Sigrid admitted. Anything to gain time! "We had . . . this sort of goal . . . in mind—a free enterprise economy at a stage of pioneering and expansion—but there are so many clusters. . . . After visiting only two, though, we heard rumours about yours." A measure of strength returned. She straightened. The Forsi were apparently even more dull-nosed than humans, which gave some hope. "Do you think you can get away with this crime?" she blustered. "Let me go now and I'll make no complaint against you."

The goblins chuckled.

"Best we start with you at once," the leader told her. "If we can reach the spaceport before the evening rush, so you are not noticed by anyone, our ship can ask immediate clearance and lift within an hour. Otherwise we may have to wait for the same time tomorrow."

Sigrid shivered in the bitter air.

"What harm have we done?" she protested. "We sha-Terra don't threaten anybody. We're alone, planetless, we can't have children or—"

The chief signalled his waldo operators, who returned to their control boards.

"We hope to leave within a few years," Sigrid pleaded. "Can't you realize our situation? We've made no secret of it. Our planet is dead. A few ships with our own kind—males—are scattered we know not where in the galaxy. We fled this far to be safe from Earth's unknown enemy. Not to become powerful here, not even to make our home here, but to be safe. Then we had to make a living—"

"Which you have done with an effectiveness that has already overthrown many calculations," said a Forsi dryly.

"But, but, but listen! Certainly we're trying to become rich. As rich as possible. But not as an end in itself. Only as a means. When we have enough wealth, we can hire enough ships . . . to scour the galaxy for other humans. That's all, I swear!"

"A most ingenious scheme," the chief nodded. "It might succeed, given time."

"And then . . . we wouldn't stay here. We wouldn't want to. This isn't our civilization. We'd go back, get revenge for Earth, establish ourselves among familiar planets. Or else we'd make a clean break, go far beyond every frontier, colonize a wholly new world. We are not your competitors. Not in the long run. Can't you understand?"

"Even the short run is proving unpleasant for us," the chief said. "And as for long-range consequences, you may depart, but the corporate structure you will have built up—still more important, the methods and ideas you introduce—those will remain. Forsi cannot cope with them. So, you will now go with us through the rear exit. A private gravsled is waiting to bring us to the spaceport."

The waldo operators put arms and legs into the transmission sheaths, head into the control hoods. A robot reached out for Sigrid.

She dodged. It lumbered after her. She fled across the room. No use yelling. Every apartment in this city was soundproofed. The second robot closed in from the other side. They herded her towards a corner.

"Behave yourself!" The chief rose and rapped on the table. "There are punishments—"

She didn't hear the rest. Backed against a wall, she saw the gap between the machines and moved as if to go through it. The robots glided together. Sigrid spun on her heel and went to the right. An arm scooped after her. It brushed her hair, then she was past.

The robots whirled and ran in pursuit. She snatched up a stool and threw it. The thing bounced off metal. Useless, useless. She scuttled towards the doors. A robot got there first. She ran back. A Forsi left his seat and intercepted her.

Cold arms closed about her waist. She snarled and brought her knee sharply up. Vulnerable as a man, the creature yammered and let go. She sprang by him. The stool lay in her path. She seized it and brought it down on a bald head at the table. The *thonk!* was loud above their voices.

Up on to the table top she jumped. The chief grabbed at her ankles. She kicked him in one bulging eye. As he sagged, cursing his pain, she stepped on his shoulder and leaped down behind.

Running faster than human, the robots were on either side of her. She dropped to the floor and rolled beneath the table. The Forsi shouted and scrambled. For a minute or more they milled around, interfered with the robots. She saw their thick grey legs churn and stamp.

Someone bawled an order. The Forsi moved out of the way. One robot lifted the table. Sigrid rose as it did. The other approached her. She balanced, waiting. As it grabbed, she threw herself forward. The hands clashed together above her head. She went on her knees before its legs. There was just room to squeeze between. She twisted clear, bounced to her feet, and pelted towards the rear exit.

No doubt it wouldn't open for her—How long had she dodged and ducked? How long could she? The breath was raw in her gullet.

The front door spoke. "Open!" Sigrid yelled, before anyone could shout a negative. And it was not set to obey only a few beings. It flung wide.

Four sha-Eyzka stood there. And Alexandra, Alexandra. She had the only gun. It flew to her hand.

The robots wheeled and pounced. A bullet ricocheted off one breastplate with a horrible bee-buzz. Alexandra's face twisted in a grin. She held her ground as the giants neared, aimed past them, and fired twice. The operators slumped. The robots went dead.

The Forsi leader howled a command. Recklessly, his followers attacked. Two more were shot. Then they were upon Alexandra and her companions in a wave.

Sigrid ran around the mêlée. To the control panels! She yanked one body from its seat. The sheaths and masks didn't fit her very well, and she wasn't used to waldo operation in any event. However, skill wasn't needed. Strength sufficed. The robot had enough of that. She began plucking grey forms off her rescuers and disabling them. The fight was soon over.

An Eyzka called the police corporation while the others secured the surviving Forsi. "There's going to be one all-time diplomatic explosion about this, my dear," Alexandra panted. "Which . . . I think . . . Terran Traders, Inc., can turn to advantage."

Sigrid grinned feebly. "What a ravening capitalist you have become!" she said.

'I have no choice, have I? You were the one who first proposed that we turn merchants." The Yugoslav girl hefted her gun. "But if violence is to be a regular thing, *I* will make a suggestion or two. Not that you did badly in that department, either. When you weren't home, and Taltla said the hallway reeked of cologne, I knew something was amiss. Whoo, what a dose you gave yourself! A week's baths won't clean it all off. These lads I got together to help me could even follow where you'd gone by sled, you left such a scent." She looked at the sullen prisoners. Her head shook, her tongue clicked. "So they thought to get tough with us? Poor little devils!"

IX

Waken, all of King Volmer's men!
Buckle on rusted swords again,
Fetch in the churches the dust-covered shield.
Blazoned by trolls and the beasts of the field.
Waken your horses, which graze in the mould,
Set in their bellies the rowels of gold,
Leap towards Gurre town,
Now that the sun is down!

—Jacobsen

RAIN CAME from the north on a wind that bounced it smoking off roofs and flattened the snake trees on runnelling mud. Lightning glared above, stark white and then a blink of darkness; thunder banged through all howls and gurgles. The Lobo crawled into their beehive huts and wallowed together, each heap a family. Not even the Tall Masters

115

could demand they work in such weather! Only Dzhugach Base, domes and towers and sky-pointing ships, held firm in the landscape.

During the past weeks, Donnan had come to know the Kandemirians well enough to suspect a certain symbolism when Koshcha of the Zhanbulak told him over the intercom that the paragrav detector would receive a free-space test as scheduled. He saluted and switched off the speaker. "They're on their way, boys," he said "Twitter-tweet"—he meant one of the natives that did menial work around the place; a few spoke Uru— "remarked to me that it's raining cats and dogs, which on this planet means tigers and wolverines. But our chums aren't going to let that stop them."

He saw how the forty men grew taut. Howard moistened his lips, O'Banion crossed himself, Wright whispered something to Rogers, Yule in his loneliness on the fringe clamped fists together till the knuckles stood white. "Calm down, there," Donnan said. "We don't want to give the show away yet. Maybe no one here savvies English or can read a human expression, but they aren't fools."

Goldspring wheeled forward the detector, haywired ugliness on a lab cart. The biggest chunk of luck so far in this caper, Donnan thought, had been Koshcha's agreement to let them have one model here in their living-quarters to tinker with when Goldspring and his assistants were not actually in the base workshop. To be sure, the human request was reasonable. In the present state of the art, an interferometric detector was not a standardized jigsaw puzzle but a cranky monster made to work by cut and try. So the more time Goldspring had to fool around with such gadgets, the sooner he would get at least one of the lot functioning. This was the more true as the detectors being built here were much scaled up from the one he had used aboard the *Hrunna*.

As for the rest of the men, especially those not qualified to help in the workshop, they also benefited. Without something like this to think about and discuss, they might have gone stir crazy. No hazard was involved to the Kandemirians, no fantasy about the prisoners turning a micro-ultra-filtmeter into a Von Krockmeier hyperspace lever and escaping. Koshcha's physics team knew precisely what each electronic component was and for what mathematical reason it was there. No Earthling touched any equipment until Goldspring's lectures had convinced some very sharp minds that his theory was sound and his circuit diagrams valid. Furthermore, the prison suite was bugged.

Nevertheless, Koshcha might well have refused Donnan's request for parts to build a detector in the living-quarters. If so, Donnan's plan for crashing out would not have been completely invalidated, but the escape of the entire human crew would have been impossible.

Not that it looked very probable yet.

Goldspring's face glistened with sweat. "Ready to go, then . . . I think," he said. The few trained men who were supposed to accompany him into space today gathered close around, apart from the rest. Donnan joined their circle. His grin at them was the merest rictus. His own mouth was dry and he couldn't smell their sweat, he stank so much himself. His awareness thrummed.

But he functioned with an efficiency that a distant part of him admired. The technicians around the cart shielded it from the telecom eye. Goldspring unbolted a cover on the awkward machine. Donnan plunged his hands into its guts.

A minute later he nodded and stepped back. Goldspring returned the cover. Ramri joined Donnan, taking the man's arm and standing close to hide the bulge under the coat.

"Do you truly believe we shall succeed?" the Monwaingi fluted in English.

"Ask me again in an hour," Donnan said. Idiotically, since they had discussed this often before: "You sure you can operate such a boat, now? I mean, not just that it's built for another species than yours, but the whole layout'll be new. The manuals will be in a foreign language. Even the instruments, the meters—Kandemirian numbers are based on twelve, aren't they?—I mean—"

"I believe *we* can do it," Ramri said gently. "Spaceships from similar planets do not differ that much from each other. They cannot. As for nagivation tables and the like, I do have some familiarity with the Erzhuat language." His feathers rose, so that blueness rippled along them. "Carl-my-friend, you must not be frightened. This is a moment for glory."

"Tell me that, too, later on." Donnan tried to laugh. He failed.

"No, can you not understand? Had there been no such hope as this, I would have ended my own life weeks ago. So nothing can be lost today. In all the years I spent on Earth as an agent of the Tanthai traders, I never grasped why the onset of hope should terrify you humans more than despair does."

"Well, we, uh, we just aren't Monwaingi, I reckon."

"No. Which is best. What a splendid facet of reality was darkened when Earth came to an end! I do not think there can ever have been a nobler concept than your own country's constitutional law. And chess, and Beethoven's last quartets, and—" Ramri squeezed the arm he held. "No, forgive me, my friend, your facet is not gone. It shall shine again . . . on New Earth."

They said no more. A thick stillness descended on the room.

After some fraction of eternity, the main door opened. Four soldiers glided in and posted themselves, two on either side, guns covering the men. Koshcha and half a dozen associates followed. The chief physicist gestured imperiously. "Come along, you," he snapped in Uru. "Goldspring's party. The rest get back there."

Donnan and Ramri advanced. The Kandemirians seemed endlessly tall. They've only got thirteen or fourteen inches on you, Donnan told himself under the noise in his head. That don't signify. The hell it doesn't. Longest fourteen inches I ever looked up. He cleared his throat. "I'd like to come too," he said. "In fact, I'd like to take our full complement along."

"What nonsense is this?" Koshcha stiffened.

Donnan came near enough to buttonhole the scientist, if a buttonhole had been there. "We're all technically trained," he argued. "We're used to working as a team. We've all fiddled around with the detector you let us build in here, talked about it, made suggestions. You'd find our whole bunch useful."

"Crammed into a laboratory flitter with my own personnel?" Koshcha scoffed. "Don't be a clown, Donnan."

"But damn it, we're going off our trolleys in here. The agreement was we'd switch sides and work for your planet. Well, we've done so. We've produced several detectors in your workshops and one in here. Their ground tests have been satisfactory. So when are you going to start treating us like allies instead of prisoners?"

"Later, I tell you, no arrangements——"

Donnan pulled the gun from beneath his coat and jammed it into Koshcha's belly. "Not a move!" he said in a near whisper. "Don't so much as twitch a tendril. Anybody."

The unhuman eyes grew black with pupil dilation. One soldier tried to swing his rifle around from its inward aim. Ramri kicked; three talons struck with bone-breaking force. The weapon clattered down as the soldier doubled in anguish.

Donnan could only hope that his men, crowding near, screened his tableau from the telecom eye with their backs—and that the Kandemirians in the warden's office were too confident, by now, to watch the spy screen continuously. "Drop your guns or Koshcha dies," he said.

Like most nomadic units, this one was organized by clans; the technicians and their bodyguards were blood relatives. And the leader of the group was also a senior Zhanbulak. Furthermore, Donnan had plainly thumbed his rifle to continuous-fire explosive. Before he could be shot, he would have chewed up several Kandemirians. The three soldiers who still covered his men with their own guns might have threatened to shoot them. But the soldiers were too shaken. Donnan heard their rifles fall. "About face," he commanded. "To the hangar . . . march!"

The Kandemirians stumbled out the door, looking stunned, and down a long, bare, coldly lit corridor. Donnan paced them at the rear, his gun in the crook of an arm. His crew surged after.

Koshcha's mind must be churning below that red ruff. How had the Terrestrials got a weapon? By what treachery, through what rebellious Loho or (oh, unthinkable!) what bribed clansman? Maybe in another minute or two someone would guess the answer. But that would be too late. Four men behind Donnan had guns now, dropped by the guards.

Four real guns.

Hand-make a new type of device. Complicate your problem by building it on a larger scale than before. Your circuits will remain essentially the same, and understandable. Your captors will issue you precisely those conductors, resistors, amplifiers and other components that you can prove you need. But who pays attention to the chassis? It is only a framework, supporting and enclosing the instrument's vitals. You may have to adjust this or that electronic part to compensate for its properties, but not by much. The chassis is negligible.

So if anyone asks why you are turning out a slim hollow cylinder on lathe and drill beam, explain casually that it is to strengthen the frame and hold a sheaf of wires. If your angle braces have odd shapes, this must be dictated by the geometry of the layout. If a hole in the cabinet, accidentally burnt through, is repaired by bolting a scrap of metal over it, who will notice the outline of that scrap? And so on and so on.

Come the moment of untruth, you quickly remove those certain parts from the chassis, fit them together, and have quite a good imitation of a cycle rifle.

If the scheme had failed, Donnan wasn't sure what he would have done. Probably have yielded completely and let Kandemir have his soul. As matters had developed, though, he was committed. If his plan went up the spout now, his best bet was to try and get himself killed.

Fair enough, he thought.

They started down a ramp. Two non-coms going the other way saluted. They couldn't hide their surprise at the human crowd in the officers' wake. "Let 'em have it, boys." Donnan said."Quiet, though."

A gun burped. The non-coms fell like big, loose-jointed puppets. Their blood was darker red than a man's. Donnan wondered momentarily if they had wives and kids at home.

"No, you murderer!" Koshcha stopped, half turning around. Donnan jerked the fake gun at him.

"March!"

They hustled on. There was little occasion, especially today, for anyone to use the flitter hangar. But on arrival—

Two sentries outside the gate slanted their rifles forwards.

"Halt! By what authority—" A blast from behind Donnan smashed them to fragments, smeared across the steel panels.

A Kandemirian prisoner roared, wheeled, and sprang at him. He gave the fellow his gun butt in the mouth. The Kandemirian went to one knee, reached forward and caught Donnan's ankle. They rolled over, grappling for the throat. Rifles coughed above them. An alarm began to whistle.

"The door's locked!" Ramri shouted. "Here, give me a weapon, I shall try to blast the lock."

The Kandemirian's smashed mouth grinned hatred at Donnan. The giant had got on top of him, twelve fingers around the windpipe. Donnan felt his brain spin towards blackness. He set his own wrists between the enemy's and heaved outwards with all the force of his shoulders. The black nails left bloody tracks as they were pulled free. Donnan slugged below the chest. Nothing happened. The Kandemirians didn't keep a solar plexus there.

He climbed to a sitting position by means of the clansman's tunic. The unfairly long arms warded him off. Thumbs sought his eyeballs. He ducked his head and pummelled the enemy's back.

Ramri left the sprung door in a single jump. One kick by a spurred foot opened the Kandemirian's rib cage. Donnan crawled from beneath. The alarm skirled over his heart-beats and his gulps for air.

"Hurry!" Howard shouted. "I hear 'em coming!"

The men poured through, into the cavernous hangar. Rank upon rank of small spacecraft gleamed almost as far as you could see. One was aimed roofwards in its cradle. The airlock stood open. A fight ramped around there, as the humans attacked its crew.

"I must have a few moments aboard to study the controls," Ramri said to Donnan, who lurched along on Goldspring's arms. "I know that one alone can manage a flitter in an emergency, but I am not certain how, in this case."

"We'll oblige you," Lieutenant Howard said. He called out orders. A good man, Donnan thought remotely; a damn good second-rank officer. His trouble had been trying to be skipper. Well, I'm not showing up any too brilliantly in that post either, am I?

A flying wedge of humans formed behind Howard. He had a gun. The rest had mass and desperation. They charged over the gang ramp and through the lock. The Kandemirians gave way—no choice—and tried to follow. The remaining Terrestrials fell on them afresh. Bullets raved.

"Let's get you aboard also, captain," Goldspring said. "Get everybody aboard. We haven't much time."

"Haven't any time," said Yule. "Here comes the garrison."

A few giants loomed at the sagging door. Slugs hailed around them. One fell, the other two ran from sight. "They'll be back," Donnan mumbled. "And there are more entrances than this. We need a few men to hunker down—the boats and cradles'll provide cover—and stand 'em off till we can lift. Gimme a gun, somebody. Volunteers?"

"Here," said Yule. A curious, peaceful look descended on his face. He snatched away the rifle which O'Banion had handed Donnan.

"Gimme that," Donnan choked.

"Get him aboard, Mr. Goldspring," Yule ordered. "He'll be needed later on."

Donnan clung to the physicist, too dizzy and beaten to protest. Goldspring regarded Yule for a second or two. "Whoever stays behind will probably be killed," he said slowly.

Yule spat. "I know. So what? Not that I'm any goddamn hero. But I'm a man."

"I'll design a weapon in your name," Goldspring said. "I thought of several while we were here."

"Good." Yule shoved him towards the lock. Three other men joined the rearguard. They posted themselves wherever they could find shelter. Presently they were alone, except for the dead.

Then, from several directions, the Kandemirians poured in. Explosions echoed under the roof.

Thermite blazed and ate. Goldspring risked his life to appear in the airlock and wave: *We can go now.*

"You know damn well my squad 'ud never make it," Yule shouted at him. "Shut that door, you idiot, and let us get back to work!" He wasn't sure if Goldspring could hear through the racket or see through the smoke and reek. But after a few seconds the lock closed. The flitter sprang from its cradle. Automatic doors opened above. Rain poured in, blindingly, for the moment that the flitter needed to depart.

—"We are safe," Ramri sighed.

"From everything but missiles and half the Grand Fleet, trying to head us off before we make an interference fringe," Donnan said grimly.

"What can they do but annihilate us?"

"Uh . . . yes. I see what you mean. Safe."

Ramri peered into the viewscreen. Lightning had given way to the stars. "My friend," he said, and hesitated.

"Yes?" Donnan asked.

"I think—" The troubled voice faded. "I think we had best change course again." The Monwaingi touched controls. They were depending on random vectors to elude pursuit. After all, space was big and the Kandemirian defences had been designed to halt things that moved planetwards, not starwards.

"That isn't what you were getting at," Donnan said.

"No." Decision came. Ramri straightened until his profile jutted across the constellations. "Carl-my-friend, I offer apology. But many years have passed since I saw my own people. I am the only one here who can read enough Erzhuat to pilot this vessel. I shall take us to Katkinu."

"Shucks, pal," Donnan said. "I expected that. Go right ahead." His tone roughened. "I'd like a few words with your leaders anyway."

X

A nation, to be successful, should change its tactics every ten years.

—*Napoleon*

FOR A MOMENT, when his gaze happened to dwell on the horizon, Donnan thought he was home again. Snowpeaks afloat in serene blue, purple masses and distances that shaded into a thousand greens as the valley floor rolled nearer, the light of a yellow sun and the way cloud shadows raced across the world, wind blustering in sky and trees, woke him from a nightmare in which Earth had become a cinder. He thought confusedly that he was a boy, footloose in the Appalachians; he had slept in a hayloft and this dawn the farmer's daughter kissed him goodbye at the mailbox, which was overgrown with morning glory. . . . A night that stung descended on his eyes.

Ramri glanced at him, once, and then concentrated on steering the ground-runner. After his years on Earth and in space, the avian found it a little disconcerting to ride on the chair-like humps of a twenty-foot, eight-legged mammaloid and control it by touching spots that were nerve endings. Such vehicles had been obsolescent on Katkinu even when he left. The paragrav boats that flitted overhead were more to Tanthai liking. But today he and Donnan where bound from his home to the Resident, who was of the Laothaung Society. Paying a formal call on a high official from *that* culture, and arriving in dead machinery, would have been an insult.

After a while, Donnan mastered himself. He fumbled with his pipe. The devil take tobacco rationing . . . just now . . . especially since Ramri assured him that the creation of an almost identical leaf would be simple for any genetic engineer on any Monwaingi planet. When he had it lit, he paid close attention to nearby details. Katkinu was not Earth, absolutely not, and he'd better fix that squarely in his head.

Even to the naked eye, the similarities of grass and foliage and flowers were superficial. Biochemical analysis showed how violently those life forms differed from himself. He had needed antiallergen shots before he could even leave the space flitter and step on Katkinuan soil. The odours blown down the wind were spicy, mostly pleasant, but like nothing he had ever known at home. Along this road (paved, if that was the word, with a thick mossy growth, intensely green) walked blue parrot-faced creatures carrying odd-shaped tools and bundles. Houses, widely scattered, each surrounded by trees and a brilliant garden, were themselves vegetable: giant growths shaped like barrel cacti, whose hollow interiors formed rooms of nacreous beauty. A grain-field was being cultivated by shambling octopids, mutated and bred for one purpose—like the thing on which he rode.

Yeh, he thought, I get the idea. These people aren't human. Even Ramri, who sings Mozart themes and has Justice Holmes for a hero—Ramri, about the most *simpático* guy I ever met—he's not human. He came back to his wife and kids after eight years or whatever it was, and he might simply have stepped around the corner for a beer.

Of course, Donnan's mind rambled on, that's partly culture. The Tanthai civilization puts a premium on individualism. The family isn't quite that loose in the other Monwaingi Societies, I reckon. But no human anywhere could have been that casual about a long separation, when obviously they're an affectionate couple. Ramri did say to me once, his species doesn't have a built-in sex drive like ours. When the opposite sex is out of sight, it really and truly is out of mind. Nevertheless—!

Or was I just missing the nuances? Did a few

words and a hug accomplish as much for Ramri and his wife as Alison and I could've got across in a week?

If I'd ever given Alison the chance.

He said quickly: "You'd better put me straight on the situation here. I'm still vague on details. As I understand your system, each planet colonized by your people has a governor-general from Monwaing, the mother world. Right?"

Ramri scratched his crest. "Well, no," he answered. "Or yes. A semantic question. And not one that can ever be resolved fully. After all, since Resident Wandwai is a Laothaungi, he speaks another language from mine, lives under different laws and customs, enjoys art forms strange to me. So what he understands by the term *Subo*— 'Resident', you say—is not identical with what a Tanthai like myself understands. Such differences are sometimes subtle, sometimes gross, but always present. He doesn't even use the same phonetic symbols."

"Huh? I never realized—I mean, I assumed you'd at least agree on an alphabet and number signs."

"Oh, no. Some Societies do, to be sure. But Laothaung, for instance, which makes calligraphy a major art, finds our Tanthai characters hideous. All Monwaingi writing does go from left to right, like English or Erzhuat, and not from right to left like Japanese or Vorlakka. But otherwise there is considerable variation from Society to Society. Likewise with mathematical ideograms. . . . Naturally, any cultured person tries to become familiar with the language and traditions of the more important foreign Societies. Wandwai speaks fluent Tanthai. But I fear I am quite ignorant of Loathaungi. My interests were directed elsewhere than the arts. In that, I am typical of this planet Katkinu. We Tanthai have taken far more interest in physical science and technology than most other Monwaingi civilizations. Some, in fact, have found such innovations extremely repugnant. But physics proved welcome to the Tanthai world-view."

"Hey," Donnan objected, "your people must have had some physics even before the galactics discovered Monwaing. Otherwise you could never have developed these systematic plant and animal mutations, let alone build spaceships yourselves."

"Yes, yes. There was considerable theoretical physics on Monwaing when the Uru explorers arrived. And it found a certain amount of practical application. The emphasis lay elsewhere, though. Your recent development on Earth was almost a mirror image of Monwaing two centuries past. You knew far more biological theory than you had yet put into engineering practice because your intellectual and economic investments were already heaviest in physical, inanimate matter. Our situation was the reverse."

"This is getting too deep for me," Donnan said. "I'll never comprehend your set-up. Especially as it was before you got space travel. I can see your different civilizations these days, scattering out to new planets where they aren't bothered by unlike neighbours. But how did totally different cultures ever co-exist in the same geographic area?"

"They still do, on Monwaing," Ramri said. "For that matter, several other Societies have planted colonies of their own here on Katkinu. Tantha merely has a majority." He pointed out a cluster of buildings, tall garishly coloured cylinders erected in steel and plastic, half a mile off the road. The avians walking between them wore embroidered jackets over their feathers. "That is a Kodau village, for example. I suppose you could best describe them as religious communists. They don't bother us and we don't bother them. I admit, such peace was slowly and painfully learned. If we never had major wars on Monwaing, we had far more local flare-ups than you humans. But eventually methods were developed for arbitrating disputes. That is what a nation was, with us—a set of public technical services, jointly maintained. And peace-keeping is only another technology, no more mysterious than agronomy or therapeutics. Once that idea caught on, a planetary government was soon organized."

He cocked an eye at Donnan, decided the man still needed to be soothed, and continued reciting the banal and obvious:

"To be sure, as proximity and mutual influence grew, the various cultures were losing their identities. Space travel came as a saviour. Now we have elbow room again. We can experiment without upsetting the balance between ourselves and our intermingled neighbour Societies. And fresh, new influences have come from space to invigorate us.

"Really, Carl-my-friend, despite our many talks in the past, I do not believe you know what an impact Terrestrial ideas have had on the Monwaingi. You benefitted us not simply by selling us raw materials and machine parts and so on— your engineers, in effect, working cheaper than ours for the sake of learning modern techniques— but you presented us with your entire philosophy. Tantha in particular had looked upon itself as rather reactionary and anti-scientific. You made us realize that technology *per se* did not conflict with our world-view, only biological technology. The inherent callousness of manipulating life." His gesture at the beast they rode was eloquent, like a man's grimace.

"That ruthlessness was spreading into the psychotechnical field too," he went on. "In other Societies, talk was being heard of adjusting the personality to suit—like the genes of any domestic animal! Such concepts alarmed us. Yet if we Tanthai failed to keep pace with innovation, we would dwindle, impotent. . . . Then, suddenly, on Earth and especially in America, we found a socio-economic system based on physics rather than biology. It was less subtle, perhaps, than the traditional Monwaingi approach; but potentially it was of far greater power . . . and humaneness. We were eager to adopt what we had seen. Do you know, even I am astounded at how far change has progressed on Katkinu in my absence. Why, in my own house, fluorescent panels! When I left, glowfly globes were still the only artificial light. And that is a trivial example. I tell you, your species has inspired my Society."

"Thanks," Donnan grunted.

Humans couldn't have had such a history, he thought. Maybe the vilayet system of the Ottoman Empire had approximated it, but not very closely. No human culture had ever experimented with radical social change and not paid a heavy emotional price. Think how many psychiatrists had been practising in the U.S.A., or walk down any American street and count on one hand the people who actually looked as if they enjoyed life. To a Monwaingi, though, change came naturally. They didn't need roots the way men did. Possibly their quasi-instinctive rituals of music and dance, universal and timeless, gave the individual that sense of security and meaningfulness which a human got from social traditions.

No help here for the last Earthmen, Donnan thought wearily. We've got to find our own planet and start up our own way of life again. If we can have kids who'll get some benefit from our trouble. Otherwise, to hell with it. Too much like work.

Ramri made an embarrassed, piping noise. "Er . . . we seem to have wandered over half the galaxy in this discussion," he said. "You started asking what Resident Wandwai and his staff do. Well, he represents the mother world, and thus the whole coalition of our planets and Societies.

He administers the arbitration service. And, these days, he is a military liaison officer. You know that the Kandemirian menace requires each Society to maintain spatial defence forces. The central government on Monwaing co-ordinates their activities as needed, through the Resident on each colonial world."

Also, Donnan reflected, the central government on Monwaing operates some damned efficient cold-war type diplomacy, espionage, and general intriguing. Yes, I do think we had to come to one of these planets and talk with one of their big wheels.

"I know each Society has spokesmen on Monwaing," he said, "but does each one have an equal voice in policy?"

"A shrewd question," Ramri approved. "No, certainly not. How could the primitivistic Maudwai or the ultra-pacifistic Bodantha find ways to keep Kandemir from gobbling up our scattered planets? The handling of foreign affairs and defense gravitates naturally towards members of the most powerful cultures, notably Laothaung and Thesa. We Tanthai are not unrepresented; still, we tend to be explorers and traders rather than admirals and ambassadors. . . . You needn't worry about etiquette or protocol today. Resident Wandwai won't expect you to know such fine points. Talk as plainly as you wish. He was so quick to grant your request for an interview that I am sure he is also anxious for it."

Donnan nodded and puffed his pipe in silence.

He couldn't think of anything else to say, and by now, like his whole crew, had learned patience. If they must zigzag clear into the Libra region, a hundred light-years closer to Earth than Vorlak was, and then cool their heels for days or weeks in the Monwaingi sector of space, why quibble over the extra hours this beastie took to carry him where he was going? The time wasn't really wasted, even. At least, Goldspring and his helpers were drafting some gadgets with awesome potentialities.

Sooner or later, if he didn't get killed first, Donnan would find who had murdered Earth and exact a punishment. But no hurry about that. He smoked, watched the landscape go by, and thought his own thoughts. Now and then, as on this ride today, he had some bad moments; but in general, he had begun to be able to remember Earth with more love than pain.

The trill jarred him to alertness. "We approach."

He stared about. The ground-runner was passing through an avenue of grotesquely pollarded trees, whose shapes kept altering as the wind tossed and roared in them. On either side lay terraced gardens whose forms and hues were like some he recognized from dreams. Directly ahead rose an outsize building . . . no, a grove of housetrees, vines, hedges, cascading from a matted-together roof to a fluidly stirring portico. The music that wailed an alien scale seemed to originate within those live walls. He had seen nothing like this on Katkinu. But naturally, if the Resident belonged to a different culture from the Tanthai—

A dwarfish being took charge of the ground-runner. The being's eyes were vacant and it could only respond to Ramri's simplest commands. Another organic machine; but Donnan was shocked at its obviously Monwaingi descent. Planned devolution went rather further than chattel slavery had ever done on Earth. No wonder the Tanthai wanted to get away from biotechnology.

He climbed down the vehicle's extended foreleg and followed Ramri into the portico. Three soldiers stood on guard, armed with tommy guns adapted from a Terrestrial pattern as well as with fungus grenades. Ramri and they exchanged intricate courtesies. One of them conducted the visitors along a rustling archway, where sunlight came and went in quick golden flecks, and so to an office.

That room was more familiar, its walls the mother-of-pearl grain of dukaung wood, the desk and sitting-frame like any furniture in Ramri's home. But Donnan could not recognize the calligraphic symbols burned into the ceiling. Resident Wandwai of Laothaung made a stately gesture which sent Ramri into a virtual dance. Donnan stood aside, watching his host. Wandwai belonged to a different race as well as another civilization. His feathers were almost black, eyes green, beak less strongly curved and body stockier than Ramri's. Besides the usual purse at the neck, he wore golden bands twining up his shanks.

Formalities past, the Resident offered Ramri a cigar and lit one for himself. He invited Donnan to sit on top of the desk while he and the space pilot relaxed in frames. "I wish I could give you refreshment, captain," he said in fluent Uru. "But poisoning would be poor hospitality."

"Thanks anyway," Donnan said.

"Since the first news of your arrival here, I have been eager to see you," Wandwai continued. "However, custom forced me to wait until you requested this meeting. My custom, I mean: it would have been impolite for a Tanthai not to issue an invitation. In the absence of knowledge about your own preferences, I decided to abide by Laothaungi usage."

"I should think military business would take precedence over company manners," Donnan said.

"Military? Why so? Earth never gained any intrinsic military importance."

Donnan swallowed hurt and anger. A Tanthai wouldn't have spoken so cruelly. Doubtless Wandwai didn't realize—yes, the Laothaungi having a biotechnical orientation, they would indeed be more hardboiled than average—"We escaped from Kandemir's main advance base," the human pointed out. "Didn't you expect we'd have information?" He paused, hoping for an impressive effect. "Like the fact that Earth *was* getting a bit involved in the war."

"I presume you refer to the pact between Vorlak and that one Terrestrial nation. Really, captain, we knew about that before the papers were even

signed. Monwaingi agents were everywhere on
your planet, remember." Wandwai stopped and
considered his words. Donnan wished he could
read expressions or interpret shadings of tone.
"We did not like that treaty," the Resident admitted. "The eventual Kandemirian response to
such provocation could be ominous to us, whose
scattered planets have an Earthward flank with
no defence or buffer in between. We withdrew
as many of our people from Earth as we could.

"I heard about that withdrawal from some of
Ramri's friends the other day," Donnan said rather
grimly.

"Not that we expected immediate trouble in
that area," Wandwai said. "But it seemed well to
play safe . . . especially since the coming upset of
the uneasy power balance among Terrestrial nations might bring on a general internecine war. I
regret that so few Tanthai listened to the central
government's warnings and came home before
Earth perished. Other cultures had fewer but
wiser people there."

You arrogant bastard! Donnan flared in himself.

Wandwai disarmed him by letting the cigar
droop in his delicate fingers and saying at once,
low and like a threnody: "Forgive any unintentional
offence on my part, captain. I know, to a very
small degree, what a sorrow you have suffered.
Can we Monwaingi in any way offer help or
consolation, call on us as your first and best friends.
The news that Earth had been sterilized sent a
wave of horror through us. No one believed the

Kandemirian denial of guilt. The Monwaingi coalition has, ever since, been aiding Vorlak far more heavily than before. Independent planets such as Unya and Yann tremble on the brink of declaring war; one hopeful sign that Kandemir can be defeated will decide them. Vassal worlds like T'sjuda have seen local revolts, which can probably be developed into full-scale insurrections. You know what a threat Kandemir is. By thus stirring the whole cluster to action, Earth has not died in vain."

Something in the phrasing drew Donnan's attention. Slowly he focused his mind. He felt muscles tighten; a chill went tingling over his scalp.

"You don't, yourself, believe the nomads did it," he breathed.

"No," said Wandwai. "Of course, once Earth was gone, they seized the opportunity to interdict the Solar System by planting orbital missiles whose control code is known only to them. Who else could those weapons belong to?"

"Why'd they do that, if they didn't kill Earth in the first place?"

"When the planet has cooled, a few years hence, it will still have water, oxygen, an equable temperature. The biosphere can be rebuilt. I feel sure Kandemir plans to colonize Earth sometime in the future. But certain very recent evidence has come to our attention on Monwaing which strongly indicates they are merely seizing an opportunity which was presented to them; that they did not commit the actual murder. Frankly, we have not released the information, since general anti-Kandemirian sentiment is desirable. But you, as a human, have the right to know."

Donnan slid off the desk. He stood with legs apart, shoulders hunched, fists doubled, braced for the blow. "Have you got any notion . . . who did it?"

Ramri came to stand beside him and stare in bewilderment at the Resident. Wandwai nodded. "Yes," he said. "I have."

XI

Kine die, kinfolk die,
And so at last yourself.
This I know that never dies:
How dead men's deeds are deemed.

—*Elder Edda*

"OKAY" DONNAN SAID hoarsely. "Spit it out."

Still the Resident watched him, eyes unblinking in that motionless black head. Until: "Are you strong enough?" Wandwai asked, almost inaudible. "I warn you, the shock will be great."

"By God, if you don't quit stalling—! Sorry. Please go ahead."

Wandwai beckoned a desk-drawer to open. "Very well," he agreed. "But rather than state the case myself—I fear my cultural habits strike you as tactless—let me present the evidence.

Then you can reach your own conclusions. When I knew you were coming here, I took this item from the secret file." He extracted a filmspool. The click of his claws on the floor, the snap as he put the spool in a projector seemed unnaturally loud. "This records an interview on Monwaing itself, between Kaungtha of Thesa, interrogation expert of the naval intelligence staff attached to the central government, and a certain merchant from Xo, which you will recall is a space-faring planet still neutral in the war."

"One moment, honoured Resident," Ramri interrupted. "May I ask why—if the secret is important—you have a copy?"

"Knowing several Earth ships were absent at the time of the catastrophe, Monwaingi anticipated that one or more would seek a planet of ours," Wandwai answered. "We are the only race whose friendship they could feel certain about. Not knowing which planet, however, or exactly how the crews would react to their situation, the government provided this evidence for every office. Otherwise, refusing to believe a bald statement, the Terrestrials might have departed for an altogether different civilization-cluster." He sighed. "Perhaps you will do so anyway, captain. The choice is yours. But at least you have been given what data we had."

Ramri inhaled on his cigar, raggedly. A whiff sent Donnan spluttering to one side but he never took his eyes off the projector. With a whirr, a cube of light sprang into existence. After a moment, quarter size, a three-dimensional scene appeared within.

Through an open window he saw a night sky aglitter with stars, two crescent moons, a rainbow arch that was the rings around Monwaing. Crystal globes in which a hundred luminous insects darted like meteors hung from the ceiling. Behind a desk sat an avian whose feathers were bluish green and who wore a golden trident on his breast. He ruffled papers in his hands, impatiently, though he never consulted them.

The being who stood before the desk was a Xoan. Donnan recognized that from pictures only; few had ever visited Earth, which lay beyond their normal sphere of enterprise. The form was centauroid, which is to say there was a quadrupedal body as big as a Shetland pony and an upright torso with arms. But iridescent skin, erectible comb on the head, face dominated by a small proboscis, removed any further resemblance to anything Earthly. The Xoan seemed nervous, shuffling his feet and twitching his trunk.

A disembodied voice sang some phrases in a Monwaingi language. Ramri whispered: "That's Thesai. 'Interview between Interrogator Kaungtha and Hordelin-Barjat, chairman of the navigation committee of the spaceship *Zeyan-12* from the planet generally known as Xo: catalogue number— Never mind. The date is—let me translate—about six months ago."

Kaungtha's replica emitted a trill or two. Then, in Uru, his voice said from the light cube: "Be at ease, Navigator. We wish you no harm. This interview is only to put on official record certain statements previously made by you."

"Under duress!" The Xoan had a ridiculous squeaky voice. "I protest the illegal detention of my ship and personnel on this planet, the grilling I have undergone, the mental distress."

"At ease, Navigator, I beg you. Your detention was perfectly in accord with ordinary interstellar practice as well as Monwaingi law. If contamination is suspected, what can we do but impose quarantine?"

"You know perfeclty well that—" Hordelin-Barjat subsided. "I understand. If I co-operate, you will give us a clean bill of health and allow us to depart. So . . . I am co-operating." Anxiously: "But this will remain secret? You do promise that. If my superiors ever learn—"

Kaungtha rustled his papers. "Yes, yes, you have our assurance. Believe me, Monwaing is as interested in discretion as Xo. You fear repercussions because of your planet's part in the affair. We much prefer to spare Xo any unfortunate consequences to reputation and livelihood, and let the blame continue to rest where it does. However, for our own guidance, we want accurate information."

Hordelin-Barjat: "But how did you ever come to suspect that we—"

Kaungtha (mildly): "The source of the original hints we got deserves the same protection as you. Not so? Let us commence, then. Your vessel belongs to the Xoan merchant fleet, correct?"

Hordelin-Barjat: "Yes. Our specialty, as a crew,

is to establish first contact with promising new markets and to conduct preliminary negotiations. We—that is—the planets where Xo has been trading for the last several generations . . . they are becoming glutted, or else so civilized they no longer import the . . . uh . . . specialized items manufactured on our world. We need fresh markets. Earth—"

Kaungtha: "Just so. After studying all the information available to you about Earth, you went there, secretly, in the *Zeyan 12*. That was approximately two years ago, correct?" (A sudden bark) "Why secretly?"

Hordelin-Barjat (shaken): "Well . . . that is . . . no wish to offend others—Monwaing already had interests on Earth—"

Kaungtha: "Nonsense! No treaty forbade competition in the Terrestrial marker. The Monwaingi confederation as a whole undertakes no obligation to protect the commercial interests of those member Societies that engage in trade. No, the secrecy was required by your tentative purpose. Explain in your own words what you had in mind."

Hordelin-Barjat: "I—that is—I mean—All those ridiculous nations and tribes there—hold-overs from the Stone-Age, and still unable to agree . . . in the face of galactic culture . . . agree on unity and global peace—"

Kaungtha: "You hoped, then, to sell one or two of those countries a highly advanced weapon that would overthrow the delicate balance of power existing on Earth. If this became known in advance to the rival nations, either preventive war would break out at once or an agreement would be reached to ban such devices. In either case, Xo would make no sale. Hence the secrecy."

Hordelin-Barjat: "I wouldn't put it just that way, officer. We had no intention—we never foresaw—I tell you, they were mad. The whole race was mad. Best they did die, before their lunacy threatened everyone else."

Kaungtha (sighing). "Spare me the rationalizations."

Hordelin-Barjat: "But, but, but you must understand—We are not murderers! Insofar as a psychology so alien could be predicted, we felt that . . . well, believe me, we had even read some of their own theoretical works, analyses of their own situation. A weapon like this had been discussed by Terrestrial thinkers in various books and journals. They felt—that is, the ultimate deterrent to agressions, a guaranteed peace—Well, if the Earthlings themselves believed such a device would have this effect, how should we know otherwise?

Kaungtha: "Some of them did. Most did not. In two decades of dealing with Terrestrials, we Monwaingi have got some insight into their thought processes. They are—were—they had more individual variability than Xoan's; more than any two members of one given Monwaingi Society." (Leaning forward, harsh tone, machine-gun rattle of papers) "You gathered those data which pleased you and ignored the rest."

Hordelin-Barjat: "I—we—"

Kaungtha: "Proceed. Which country did you sell this weapon to?"

Hordelin-Barjat: "Well actually . . .two. Not two countries exactly. Two alliances. Power blocs. Whatever they were called. We avoided the major powers. Among other reasons, they—uh—"

Kaungtha: "They had too many extra-terrestrial contacts. Word of your project might easily have leaked out to civilized planets, which might well have forbidden it. Also, being strong to begin with, the large nations would feel less menaced from every side; less persecuted; less petulant. In a word, less ready to buy your wares. Proceed."

Hordelin-Barjat: "I strongly object to your, er, cynical interpretation of our motives."

Kaungtha: "Proceed, I told you."

Hordelin-Barjat: "Uh—uh—well, our clients had to be countries that did possess some military force—space missiles and so on—and thereby might well expect to be attacked with missiles in the early stages of a war. We approached the Arabian-North African alliance for one. It felt itself being encircled as relations between Israel and the more southerly African states grew increasingly close. And then there was the Balkan alliance, under Yugoslavian leadership—suspicious of the Western countries, still more suspicious of Russia, from whose influence they had barely broken free—and sure to be a battleground if outright war ever did break out between East and West."

Kaungtha: "Let us positively identify the areas in question. You do not pronounce them very reliably, Navigator." (Projecting a political globe of Earth) "Here, here, here, here. Have I indicated the correct regions?"

Hordelin-Barjat: "Yes." (Hastily) "You realize these were second- and third-rate powers. They needed defence, not aggrandizement. What we sold them—"

Kaungtha: "Describe that briefly, please."

Hordelin-Barjat: "A set of disruption bombs. Buried deep in the planetary crust . . . and beneath the ocean beds . . . strategic locations—You are familiar with the technology. They—the bombs belonging to a given alliance—they would go off automatically. If more than three nuclear explosions above a certain magnitude occurred within the borders of any single member country . . . all those bombs would explode. At once."

Kaungtha (softly): "And would wipe the planet clean. In seconds."

Hordelin-Barjat: "Yes, humane, quick, yes. Of course, that was not the intention. Not anyone's intention. These small powers—they planned to go, oh, very discreetly, in deepest secrecy—they would approach the other governments and say, 'In the event of general war, we are doomed anyway. But now you will die with us. Therefore you must refrain from making war, ever again.' I assure you, the idea was to promulgate peace."

Kaungtha: "Did you witness the actual installation?"

Hordelin-Barjat: "No. My ship only conducted, uh, preliminary negotiations. Others came later, technicians and so on. I was informed . . . once

. . . verbally . . . that the task had been completed and payment made. But I never saw—" (Shriller than before) "I give you assurance I was as shocked as anyone to hear—not long afterward— by superiors, too—Who could have known that the whole Terrestrial species was insane?"

Kaungtha: "Have you any idea what might have happened, exactly?"

Hordelin-Barjat: "No. Perhaps . . . oh, I can't say. . . . No doubt a war did break out—regardless. If they were already on edge, those governments, then the increased tension . . . feeling this was a bluff that should be called—Or even an accident. I don't know, I tell you! Let me alone!"

Kaungtha: "That appears sufficient, Navigator. End interview."

The cube of light blanked out.

Donnan heard himself speaking in a voice not his own, "I don't believe it! I won't! Take back your lies, you—"

Ramri pushed him against the wall and held him till he stopped struggling. Wandwai gazed at the symbols burned into the ceiling as if to find some obscure comfort.

"Not murder, then," the Resident said at last. "Suicide."

"They wouldn't!"

"You may reject this evidence," said the gentle, surgical voice. "Admittedly it is not conclusive. The Xoan might have lied. Or, even if he told the truth, the Kandemirians might still have launched an attack. Especially if they, somehow, learned about those bombs. For then the destruction of Earth would be absurdly simple. A few medium-power nuclear missiles, landing within a fair-sized geographical area, would touch off the supreme explosion. But Earth herself would nevertheless have provided the means."

Donnan covered his face and sagged.

When he looked at them again, Wandwai had put the projector and spool away. "For the sake of surviving humans, captain, as well as Monwaingi policy," the Resident murmured, "I trust you will hold this confidential. Now come, shall we discuss your further plans? Despite the ecological problems, I am sure a home can be made for you within our hegemony—"

"No," said Donnan.

"What?" This time Wandwai did blink.

"No. We're heading back to Vorlak. Our ship, the rest of our people—"

"Oh, they can come here. Monwaing will arrange everything with the Dragar."

"I said no. We got a war to finish."

"Even after Kandemir is proven probably innocent?"

"I don't accept your proof. Y-y-you'll have to trot out something more solid than a reel of film. I'm going to keep on looking . . . on my own account. . . . Anyway, Kandemir did kill some of my crew. And ought to be stopped on general principles. And there's still the idea we had of making a galaxy-wide splash. I'm going. Thanks for your . . . your hospitality, guv'nor. So long."

Donnan lurched from the room.

Ramri stared after him a minute, then started

in pursuit. Wandwai, who had remained still except for slow puffs on his cigar, called: "Do you think it best we stop him?"

"No, honoured Resident," Ramri answered. "It is necessary for him to depart. I am leaving too."

"Indeed? After so long an absence from home?"

"He may need me," Ramri said, and left.

XII

Who going through the vale of misery use it for a well:
and the pools are filled with water.
They will go from strength to strength.
                          —The Book of Common Prayer

BLACK AND MOUNTAINOUS, the ancestral castle of
Hlott Luurs covered the atoll on which it was
built and burrowed deep into the rock. Sheer
walls of fused stone ended in watch-towers overlooking the fishers' huts on two neighbouring
islets, and in missile turrets commanding the sky
above. Today, as often at every latitude on Vorlak,
that sky hung low. Smoky clouds tinged with
bronze by the hidden sun flew on a wind that
whipped the sea to a grey-green restlessness.
When he stood up, Carl Donnan got a faceful of

spindrift. The air was warm, but the wind whistled and the surf boomed with a singularly cold noise.

He braced his feet against roll and lurch as Ger Nenna changed course. "We must go in by the west gate," the scholar called. "None but Dragar and the Overmaster may use the north approach." His fur gleamed with salt water; he had removed his robes to keep them dry when the boat started off from Port Caalhova. Donnan stuck to his shabby coverall and a slicker.

Pretty overbearing type, that Hlott, the man thought. Oh, sure, he's entitled to be ceremonious—president of the Council and all that. And in times like these you can't blame him for not allowing any fliers but his into this area. And his refusal to talk with me after I got back is within his rights. But when you add everything together, he's treating us humans like doormats and it has got to stop.

He put arms akimbo. The old Mauser would have been comforting on his hip today. But naturally, he wasn't allowed to bear weapons here. He couldn't even have got this interview had it not been for Ger Nenna's repeated petitions.

They passed a few fisher craft, off which commoners dived like seals to herd schools detected by sonar beams into giant scoops.

A patrol boat set down on the water and the pilot bawled a challenge. Ger identified himself and was waved on. A cliff-like wall loomed dead ahead. The portcullis was raised as Ger steered towards the entrance. Within, several boats lay docked in a basin. Ger made fast.

"Have you reconsidered your plan, captain, as I requested?" he asked.

"Uh-huh," Donnan nodded. "But I'll stick with it."

"Have you fully understood how dangerous it is? A Draga, any Draga, is supreme within his own demesne. Hlott could kill you here and there would be no lawful redress, no matter how small and poor an aristocrat he was."

"But he is not small and poor," Donnan pointed out. "He's the boss of this planet. And there lies my chance." He shrugged. The bitterness that Ger had noticed and wondered about, ever since the *Hrunna* survivors returned from Katkinu, whetted his tone. "We're the ones who're poor, we humans. Nothing to lose. And that fact can also be turned into an asset."

Ger towelled himself more or less dry and slipped the plain black robe over his head. "In the Seven Classics of Voyen," he said anxiously, "one may read, 'Many desperations do not equal one hope.' Captain, you know I favour your cause. Not from charity, but on the dim chance that you may indeed bring this wretched war to an end. Only when the interstellar situation has become stable will there be any possibility of restoring—no, not the Eternal Peace; that is gone forever—but the true Vorlakka civilization. You must never believe these swaggering Dragar represent our inherent nature as a species."

"Lord, no." Donnan shucked his slicker and

helped Ger tie an embroidered honorific sash. "In fact, pal, if the breakdown of your old universal state had not thrown up a warlord class, you'd be a pretty sorry lot. Ready? Let's go, then. Yonder guard is beginning to give us a fishy look."

They debarked and were frisked. Ger was searched nominally and with a ritual apology, Donnan like a criminal arrested for malicious hoodblinkery and aggravated conspiculation. He submitted without paying much heed. He was too busy rehearsing what—No, by God! A set speech was exactly the wrong approach. Marshal his facts, sure; but otherwise play it by ear. Keeping cool was the main thing. He was about to walk a tightrope over a pit full of razor blades.

A servant ushered them down wet, ringing corridors, up ramps worn smooth by war-like generations, and so at last to a relatively small room. It had a transparent domed roof, the walls were brightly coloured, and furniture stood about. A solarium, Donnan guessed. The guide bowed low and went out. The door shut behind him, thick and heavy.

Hlott Luurs was sprawled nude on a couch. The light from above rippled along his mahogany fur. He raised himself to one elbow and regarded them with chill eyes. No one else was present, but a web-footed, long-fanged animal, tiger size, lay at his feet. A borren, Donnan recognized. It rumbled at him until Hlott clicked his tongue for silence.

Ger Nenna advanced and bent his head. "My captain," he greeted, "dare this worm express thanks for your graciousness in heeding his prayer, or should he accept it in silence as the winter earth accepts vernal sunshine?"

"If the honourable steersman truly wants to show gratitude," said Hlott dryly, "he can spare me any future time-wastings as silly as this."

"I beg leave to assure the President that the Terrestrial captain brings news of great import."

"Yes, he does." Hlott's gaze smouldered on Donnan. Briefly, teeth flashed white in his blunt muzzle. "But I've already heard that news, you see. A good destroyer thrown away at Mayast, together with Draga Olak Faarer's life, my kinsman. Kandemir handed the secret of the new paragrav detector, as the price for sparing the flotsam lives of a few Earthlings. That is the news. And now this creature not only has the insolence to return to Vorlak—he demands we put him in charge of still more operations! Be grateful to Ger Nenna, you. I'd have blasted every last wretch of your gang before now, had he not persuaded me otherwise."

Donnan sketched an obeisance. "My captain," he said, "you agreed yourself to let us try that raid, and you were told that success wasn't guaranteed. Trying to shift the whole blame on us would be a sneaking trick."

"What?" Hlott's hackles rose. He sat straight. The borren sensed his mood and got up too, tail lashing, throat like thunder.

Donnan didn't stop to be afraid. He dared not. He kept his words loud and metallic: "Thanks for finally agreeing to hear our side of the fiasco. If you really plan to listen to me. And you'd better. This affair hasn't weakened us as you think. We're stronger than before. By 'we' I mean the *Franklin's* men; but we'll include Vorlak if you want."

The borren started towards him. Hlott called it back with a curt order. I gauged him right, then, Donnan thought, beneath his own pulse-beat and sweat. He's not so stuck on himself that he won't stop to look at facts shoved under his nose. He's not stupid at all, really; just raised in a stupid milieu.

He won't kill me simply because he gets peeved. No. He'll have excellent logical reasons.

The Draga shivered with self-restraint. "Speak, then," he said in a strangled voice. "Explain how Kandemir's possessing the new detector strengthens anyone except Tarkamat."

"Those detectors are prototypes, my captain," said Donnan, moderating his tone. "At best, a few enemy ships may now have hand-made copies. It'll take months to get them into real production. So unless we let the stalemate drag on, we haven't lost much on that account.

"The Kandemirians also have a glimpse of the theory behind the detectors. But a very partial glimpse. And they'll need time to digest their knowledge, time to see the implications and develop the possibilities. We—Arnold Goldspring and his helpers—have been thinking about this subject, off and on, for close to three years while we cruised around exploring. We've given it really concentrated attention since we returned to this cluster.

"When Goldspring and I arrived back in Vorlak from Katkinu, we found that his associates who'd stayed behind in the *Franklin* had not been idle. Thanks to Ger Nenna, who arranged access to computers and other high-powered research tools, they'd gone a long way towards developing half a dozen new applications. It's a case of genuine scientific breakthrough. Inventions based on Goldspring's principle are going to come thick and fast for a while. And we've got the jump on everybody else."

"I have been told about theoretical designs and laboratory tests," Hlott said disgustedly. "How long will it take to produce something that really works?"

"Not long, my captain." Donnan said. "That is, if a massive scientific-technological effort can be mounted. If the best Vorlakka and allied minds can work together. And that's the real technique we Earthlings have got that you don't. A feudal society like yours, or a nomadic culture like Kandemir, or a coalition of fragments like Monwaing, isn't set up to innovate on purpose. We can tell you how to organize a development project. In less than a year, we can load you for . . . for borren . . . and break the deadlock."

"So you say," Hlott growled. "Your record to date hardly justifies belief."

"Most honoured captain," Ger begged, "I have inspected the work of these people. My feeble powers were insufficient to grasp their concepts. I could only gape in awe at what was demonstrated. But scholars in the physical sciences, who have studied more deeply, assure me—"

"I don't give a curse in non-existence what they assure you, honourable steersman," Hlott answered. "If it pleases them to tinker with a new idea, let them. Something worthwhile may or may not come from it. But I am responsible for the survival of Vorlak as an independent world—and I am not going to gamble half our resources on as crazy an effort as this, masterminded by a mouthful of planetless lunatics. Go!"

Ger wrung his hands. "Noble master—"

Hlott rose to his feet. "Go." he shouted. "Before I chop you both in pieces!"

The borren snarled and crouched.

"But the noble President of Council does not realize—"

Donnan waved Ger back. "Never mind, pal," he said. "I know you hate to come right out and say this, but it's got to be done."

He planted himself solidly before the Draga and stated: "You must know I've got the backing of several Councillors. They liked what we showed them."

"Yes." Hlott relaxed enough to snort a laugh. "I have heard. Praalan, Seva, Urlant. The weakest and most impressionable members of the entire Draga class. What does that mean?"

"Exactly this, my captain," Donnan's lips bent into a sort of smile. He ticked the points off on his fingers. "One: they agree with me that if the stalemate drags on much longer, Kandemir is going to win for sure. The nomad empire has more resources in the long run. Two: once equipped with the new detectors, and the prospect of still fancier gadgets—remember, Kandemir's vassals include sedentary industrial cultures that do know how to organize weapons development—Tarkamat is going to come out looking for a showdown. So we haven't got very much time in any case. Three: if we prepare for it, we, the anti-Kandemirian alliance, can force the showdown ourselves, with a pretty fair chance of winning. Four: this is so important that Praalan and Company can't continue to support a President of the Council too bull-headed to realize simple facts."

Muscles bunched and knotted along the warlord's body. Almost, the borren went for Donnan's throat. Hlott seized its neck and expended enough temper restraining that huge mass to retort, slit-eyed but self-possessed:

"Ah, you have gone behind my back, then, and awakened intrigues against me, eh? That shall certainly be repaid you."

"I couldn't help going behind your back," Donnan snapped. "You kept it turned on me, in spite of my loudest hollering."

"Praalan, Seva, and Urlant! What can they accomplish? Let them try to force an election. Just let them dare."

"Oh, they won't by themselves, my lord. I talked 'em out of that. Persuaded them they don't, none of them, have the following—or the brains and toughness—to boss these roughneck admirals. They wouldn't last a week. However . . . they do have some resources. In cahoots, their power is not negligible. So if they were to join forces with Yentu Saetor, who is very nearly as strong as you—"

"What!"

"Got the idea? My three chums will support Yentu because I've talked them into the idea that it's more important what weapons Vorlak can get than what master Vorlak has. Yentu doesn't think too much of me and my schemes, but he's agreed to organize my project once he gets the Presidency in return for the help of my three Dragar."

Hlott cursed and struck. Donnan sidestepped the blow. The borren glided forward. Donnan closed with Hlott. He didn't try to hurt the noble, but he went into a clinch. The unhuman body struggled to break loose. Cable-strong arms threw Donnan from side to side. Teeth sought his shoulder.

"Easy, friend. Easy!" Donnan gasped. As the borren lunged, the man forced Hlott around as a shield. The great jaws nearly closed on the Draga's leg. The borren roared and drew back.

"Let's not fight, my captain," the Terrestrial said. His teeth rattled with being shaken. He bit his tongue and choked on an oath. "If . . . wait, call off your pet, will you?—if I meant you any harm, would I . . . have come here . . . and told you?"

Momentarily balked, the borren turned on Ger, who scuttled around a couch. "*Farlak!*" Hlott yelled. The beast flattened its ears and snarled. Hlott shouted again. It lay down stiff and reluctant.

Donnan let go, staggered to a couch, sat down and panted. "My . . . my captain . . . is strong as a devil," he wheezed, rather more noisily than he had to. "I couldn't . . . have held out . . . another minute."

A flicker of smugness softened the wrath of the lutrine face. Hlott said frigidly, "Your presumption deserves a very slow death."

"Pardon me, my captain," Donnan said. "You know I'm not up on your customs. Back home, in my country, one person was pretty much equal to another. I can't remember what's good manners in a society as different as this."

He rose again. "I didn't come to threaten you or any such thing," he continued, feeling how big a liar he was. "Let's say I just wanted to warn you . . . let you know what the sentiments of your colleagues are. I'd hate to see our side lose a leader as brilliant as yourself. If you'd only consider this one question of policy, you could swing back Seva, Urlant, and Praalan to your side. And—uh"—he laid a finger alongside his nose and winked—"if this move were made precisely right, the honourable Yentu could be enticed out on a nice breezy limb . . . and suddenly discover he was alone there, and you stood behind him with a bucksaw."

Hlott poised in silence. Donnan could almost watch the fury drain from him and the calculation rise. Muscle by muscle, the human allowed himself to relax. He'd probably won his case.

Practical politics was another art which had been more highly developed on Earth than it was here.

XIII

THE BATTLE OF BRANDOBAR

Annotated English version

TO THE LITERARY HISTORIAN, this ballad is notable as the first important work of art (as opposed to factual records, scientific treatises, or translations from planetary languages) composed in Uru. However, the student of military technics can best explain various passages which, couched in epical terms, convey the general sense but not the details.

The naval engagement in question was fought near the Brandobar Cluster, an otherwise undistinguished group of stars between Vorlak and Mayast. On the one side was the alliance of Vorlak, Monwaing, and several lesser races. Secret demonstrations of new weapons, combined with indignation at the ruin of Earth, had induced a number of hitherto neutral planets to declare war on Kandemir. Opposed to them was the Grand Fleet of the nomads, which included not only their clan units but various auxiliaries recruited from non-Kandemirian subjects of their empire. Their force was numerically much stronger than the attackers.

Three kings rode out on the way of war
(The stars burn bitterly clear):
Three in league against Tarkamat,
Master of Kandemir.

And the proudest king, the Vorlak lord,
(The stormwinds clamour their grief)
Had been made the servant in all but name
Of a planetless wanderer chief.

And the secondmost king was a wingless bird
(A bugle: the gods defied!)
Who leagued at last with the Vorlak lord
When the exiles were allied.

And the foremost king in all but name
(New centuries scream in birth)
Was the captain of one lonely ship
That had fled from murdered Earth.

For the world called Earth was horribly slain
(The stars burn bitterly clear)

By one unknown; but the corpse's guards
Were built on Kandemir.

The Earthlings fled—to seek revenge
(The stormwinds clamour their grief)
For ashen homes and sundered hopes
First seen in unbelief.

And haughty Vorlak spoke to them
(A bugle: the gods defied!):
"Kandemir prowls beyond our gates.
Can ye, then, stay the tide?"

And the Monwaing wisemen spoke to them
(New centuries scream in birth):
"Can ye arm us well, we will league with you,
Exiles from shattered Earth."

And the wanderer captain told the kings
(The stars burn bitterly clear):
"I have harnessed and broken to my will
Space and Force and Fear."

Tarkamat, Master of Kandemir,
(The stormwinds clamour their grief)
Laughed aloud: "I will hurl them down
Like a gale-blown autumn leaf."

And he gathered his ships to meet the three
(A bugle: the gods defied!)
As an archer rattles his arrow sheaf
And shakes his bow in pride.

Forth from their lairs, by torchlight suns,
(New centuries scream in birth)
The nomad ships came eager to eat
The wanderers from Earth.

And hard by a cluster of youthful suns
(The stars burn bitterly clear)
Known by the name of Brandobar,
They saw the enemy near.

And the three great kings beheld their foe
(The stormwinds clamour their grief)
With half again the ships they had,
Like arrows in a sheaf.

"Now hurl your vessels, my nomad lords,
(A bugle: the gods defied!)
One single shattering time, and then
Their worlds we shall bestride."

"Sleep ye or wake ye, wanderer chief,
(New centuries scream in birth)
That ye stir no hand while they seek our throats,
Yon murderers of Earth?"

Militechnicians can see from the phrasing alone, without consulting records, that the allied fleet must have proceeded at a high uniform velocity—free fall—in close formation. This offered the most tempting of targets to the Kandemirians, whose ships had carefully avoided building up much intrinsic speed and thus were more manoeuvrable.

Tarkamat moved to englobe the allies and fire on them from all sides.

"Have done, have done, my comrades twain.
(The stars burn bitterly clear)
Mine eyes have tallied each splinter and nail
In yonder burning spear.

"Let them come who slew my folk.
(The stormwinds clamour their grief)
We wait for them as waits in a sea
The steel-sharp, hidden reef."

The reference here is, of course, to the highly developed interferometric paragravity detectors with which the whole allied fleet was equipped, and which presented to the main computer in their flagship a continuous picture of the enemy dispositions. The nomads had some too, but fewer and of a less efficient model.

Now Kandemir did spurt so close
(A bugle: the gods defied!)
They saw his guns and missiles plain
Go raking for their side.

The exile captain smiled a smile
(New centuries scream in birth)
And woke the first of the wizardries
Born from the death of Earth.

Then Space arose like a wind-blown wave
(The stars burn bitterly clear)
That thunders and smokes and tosses ships
Helpless to sail or steer.

And the angry bees from the nomad hive
(The stormwinds clamour their grief)
Were whirled away past Brandobar
Like a gale-blown autumn leaf.

This was the first combat use of the space distorter. The artificial production of interference phenomena enabled the allied craft to create powerful repulsion fields about themselves, or change the curvature of the world lines of outside matter—two equivalent verbalizations of Goldspring's famous fourth equation. In effect, the oncoming enemy missiles were suddenly pushed to an immense distance, as if equipped with faster-than-light engines of their own.

Tarkamat recoiled. That is, he allowed the two fleets to inter-penetrate and pass each other. The allies decelerated and re-approached him. He acted similarly. For, in the hours that this required, his scientists had pondered what they observed. Already possessing some knowledge of the physical principles which underlay this new defence, they assured Tarkamat that it must obey the conservation-of-energy law. A ship's power plant could accelerate a missile away, but not another ship of comparable size. Nor could electromagnetic phenomena be much affected.

Tarkamat accordingly decided to match velocities and slug it out at short range with his clumsy but immensely destructive blaster cannon. He would suffer heavy losses, but the greater numbers at his command made victory seem inevitable.

Tarkamat, Master of Kandemir,
(A bugle: the gods defied!)
Rallied his heart. "Close in with them!
Smite them with fire!" he cried.

The nomad vessels hurtled near
(New centuries scream in birth)
And the second wizardry awoke,
Born from the death of Earth.

Then Force flew clear of its iron sheath.
(The stars burn bitterly clear)
Remorseless lightning cracked and crashed
In the ships of Kandemir.

And some exploded like bursting suns
(The stormwinds clamour their grief)
And some were broken in twain, and some
Fled shrieking unbelief.

Over small distances, such allied vessels as there had been time to equip with it could use the awkward, still largely experimental, but altogether deadly space-interference fusion inductor. The principle here was the production of a non-space band so narrow that particles within the nucleus itself were brought into contiguity. Atoms with positive packing fractions were thus caused to explode. Only a very low proportion of any ship's mass was disintegrated, but that usually served to destroy the vessel. More than half the Kandemirian fleet perished in a few nova-like minutes.

Tarkamat, unquestionably one of the greatest naval geniuses in galactic history, managed to withdraw the rest and re-form beyond range of the allied weapon. He saw that—as yet—it was too restricted in distance to be effective against a fortified planet, and ordered a retreat to Mayast II.

Tarkamat, Master of Kandemir,
(A bugle: the gods defied!)
Told his folk, "We have lost this day.
But the next we may abide.

"Hearten yourselves, good nomad lords,
(New centuries scream in birth)
Retreat with me to our own stronghold.
Show now what ye are worth!"

The third of those wizardries awoke
(The stars burn bitterly clear)
Born from the death of Earth. It spoke,
And the name of it was Fear.

For sudden as death by thunderbolt.

(The stormwinds clamour their grief)
Ringing within the nomad ships
Came the voice of the exile chief.

Tarkamat, Master of Kandemir,
(New centuries scream in birth)
Heard with the least of his men the words
Spoken from cindered Earth.

On the relatively coarse molecular level, the space-interference inductor was both reliable and long-range. Carl Donnan simply caused the enemy hulls to vibrate slightly, modulated this with his voice through a microphone, and filled each Kandemirian ship with his message.

"We have broken ye here by Brandobar.
(The stars burn bitterly clear)
If ye will not yield, we shall follow you
Even to Kandemir.

"But our wish is not for ashen homes,
(The stormwinds clamour their grief)
But to make you freemen once again
And not a Nomad fief.

"If ye fight, we will hurl the sky on your heads
(A bugle: the gods defied!)
If ye yield, we will bring to your homes and hearts
Freedom to be your bride.

"Have done, have done; make an end of war
(New centuries sing in birth)
And an end of woe and of tyrant rule—
In the name of living Earth!"

Tarkamat reached a cosmic interference fringe and went into faster-than-light retreat. The allies, though now numerically superior, did not pursue. They doubted their ability to capture Mayast II. Instead, they proceeded against lesser Kandemirian outposts, taking these one by one without great difficulty. Mayast could thus be isolated and nullified.

The effect of Donnan's words was considerable. Not only did this shockingly unexpected voice from nowhere strike at the cracked Kandemirian morale; it offered their vassals a way out. If these would help throw off the nomad yoke, they would not be taken over by the winning side, but given independence, even assistance. There was no immediate overt response, but the opening wedge had been driven. Soon allied agents were being smuggled onto those planets, to disseminate propaganda and organize underground movements along lines familiar to Earth's history.

Thus far the militechnic commentator. But the literary scholar sees more in the ballad. Superficially it appears to be a crude, spontaneous production. Close study reveals it is nothing of the sort. The simple fact that there had been no previous Uru poetry worth noticing would indicate as much. But the structure is also suggestive. The archaic imagery and exaggerated, often banal descriptions appeal, not to the sophisticated mind, but to emotions so primitive they are common to every space-faring race. The song could be enjoyed by any rough-and-ready space-hand, human, Vorlakka, Monwaingi, Xoan, Yannth, or whatever—including members of any other civilization-cluster where Uru was known. And, while inter-cluster traffic was not large nor steady, it did take place. A few ships a year did venture that far.

Moreover, while the form of this ballad derives from ancient European models, it is far more intricate than the present English translations can suggest. The words and concepts are simple, the meter, rhyme, assonance, and alliteration are not. They are, indeed, a jigsaw puzzle, no part of which can be distorted without affecting the whole.

Thus the song would pass rapidly from mouth to mouth, and very little changed in the process. A space-hand who had never heard of Kandemir or Earth would still get their names correct when he sang what to him was just a lively drinking song. Only those precise vocables would sound right.

So, while the author is unknown, *The Battle of Brandobar* was obviously not composed by some folkish minstrel. It was commissioned, and the poet worked along lines carefully laid down for him. This was, in fact, the *Benjamin Franklin's* message to humans throughout the galaxy.

XIV

Then I saw there was a way to Hell, even from the gates of Heaven.

—*Bunyan*

No, Sigrid Holmen told herself. Stop shivering, you fool. What is there to be afraid of?

Is it that . . . after five years . . . this is the first time I have been alone with a man? Oh, God, how cold those years were!

He wouldn't do anything. Not him, with the weather-beaten face that crinkled when he smiled, and his hair just the least bit grizzled, and that funny slow voice. Or even if he did—The thought of being grasped against a warm and muscular body made her heart miss a beat. They weren't going to wait much longer, the crews of *Europa* and *Franklin*. The half religious reverence of the first few days was already waning, companionships had begun to take shape, marriages would not delay. To be sure, even after the casualties the Americans had suffered in the Kandemirian war, they outnumbered the women. The sex ratio would get still more lopsided if—no, when! —more ships came in from wherever they were now scattered. A girl could pick and choose.

Nevertheless, murmured Sigrid's awareness, I had better choose mine before another sets her cap for him. And he wanted to see me today, all by myself. . . .

The warmth faded in her. She couldn't be mistaken about the way Carl Donnan's eyes had followed each motion she made. But something else had been present as well, or why should his tone have gone so bleak? She had sat there in the ship with the ranking officers of both expeditions, exchanging data, and described how she boarded the Kandemirian missile, and had seen his face turn stiff. Afterwards he drew her aside; low-voiced, almost furtive, he asked her to visit him confidentially next day.

But why should I be afraid? she demanded of herself again, angrily. We are together, the two halves of the human race. We know now that man will live; there will be children and hearthfires on another Earth—in the end, on a thousand or a million other Earths.

Kandemir is beaten. They have not yet admitted it, but their conquests have been stripped from them, their provinces are in revolt, they themselves requested the cease-fire which now prevails. Tarkamat spars at the conference table as bravely and skillfully as ever he did in battle, but the whole cluster knows his hope is forlorn. He will salvage what he can for his people, but Kandemir as an imperial power is finished.

Whereas we, the last few Homines sapientes, sit in the councils of the victors. Vorlak and Monwaing command ships by the thousands and troops by the millions, but they listen to Carl Donnan with deepest respect. Nor is his influence only moral. The newly freed planets, knowing that singly they can have little to say about galactic affairs, have been deftly guided into a coalition—loose indeed, but as close-knit as any such league can be among entire worlds. Collectively, they are already a great power, whose star is in the ascendant. And . . . their deliberative assembly is presided over by a human.

Why am I afraid?

She thrust the question away (but could not make herself unaware of dry mouth and fluttering pulse) as she guided her air-car on to the landing strip. Long, shingle-roofed log buildings formed a square nearby. Trees, their leaves restless in a strong wind, surrounded three sides. The fourth looked down the ridge where Donnan's headquarters stood, across the greenesses of a valley, a river that gleamed like metal, and the blue upward surge of hills on the other horizon. This was not Earth, this world called Varg, and the area Donnan occupied—like other sections lent the humans by grateful furry natives, off whom the nomad overlordship had been lifted—the area was too small to make a home. But until men agreed on what planet to colonize, Varg was near enough like Earth to ease an old pain. When Sigrid stepped out, the wind flung odours of springtime at her.

Donnan hurried from the portico. Sigrid started running to meet him, checked herself, and waited with head thrown back. He had remarked blonde hair was his favourite, and in this spilling sunlight— He extended a hand, shyly. She caught it between her own, felt her cheeks turn hot but didn't let go at once.

"Thanks for coming, Miss Holmen," he mumbled.

"Vas nothing. A pleasure." Since his French was even rustier than her English, they used the latter. Neither one considered a non-human language. She liked his drawl.

"I hope . . . the houses we turned over to you ladies . . . they're comfortable?"

"Oh, *ja, ja,*" she laughed. "Every time ve see a man, he asks us the same."

"Uh . . . no trouble? I mean, you know, some of the boys are kind of impetuous. They don't mean any harm, but—"

"Ve have impetuous vuns too." They released each other. She turned in confusion from his grey gaze and looked across the valley. "How beautiful a view!" she said. "Reminds me about Dalarna, v'en I vas a girl—do you live here?"

"I bunk here when I'm on Varg, if that's what

you mean, Miss Holmen. The other buildings are for my immediate staff and any visiting firemen. Yeh, the view is nice. But . . . uh . . . didn't you like that planet—Zatlokopa, you call it?—the one you lived on, in the other cluster? Captain Poussin told me the climate was fine."

"Vell, I say nothing against it. But thank God, ve vere too busy to feel often how lonely it vas for us."

"I, uh, I understand you were doing quite well."

"Yes. Vuns we had learned, v'at you say, the ropes, ve got rich fast. In a few more years, Terran Traders, Inc., vould have been the greatest economic power in that galactic region. Ve could have sent a thousand ships out looking for other survivors." She shrugged. "I am not bragging. Ve had advantages. Such as necessity."

"Uh-huh. What a notion!" He shook his head admiringly. "We both had the same problem, how to contact other humans and warn them about the situation. Judas priest, though, how much more elegant your solution was!"

"But slow," she said. "Ve vere not expecting to be able to do much about it for years. The day Yael Blum came back from Yotl's Nest and told v'at she had heard, a song being sung by a spaceman from another cluster—and ve knew other humans vere alive and ve could safely return here to them—no, there can only be two such days in my lifetime."

"What's the other one?"

She didn't look at him, but surprised herself by how quietly she said, "V'en my first-born is laid in my arms."

For a while only the wind blew, loud in the trees. "Yeah," Donnan said at last, indistinctly, "I told you I bunked here. But it's not a home. Couldn't be, before now."

As if trying to escape from too much revelation, she blurted, "Our problems are not ended. V'at vill the men do that don't get . . . get married?"

"That's been thought about," he answered, unwilling. "We, uh, we should pass on as many chromosomes as possible. That is, uh, well, seems like—"

Her face burned and she held her eyes firmly on the blue hills. But she was able to say for him: "Best that, in this first generation, each woman have children by several different men?"

"Uh—"

"Ve discussed this too, Carl, v'ile the *Europa* vas bound here. Some among us, like . . . oh . . . my friend Alexandra, for vun . . . some are villing to live with any number of men. Polyandry, is that the vord? So that solves part of the problem. Others like me—vell, ve shall do v'at seems our duty to the race, but ve only vant a single real husband. He . . . he vill have to understand more than husbands needed to understand on Earth."

Donnan caught her arm. The pressure became painful, but she wouldn't have asked him to let go had it been worse.

Until, suddenly, he did. He almost flung her aside. She turned in astonishment and saw he had faced away. His head was hunched between his shoulders and his fists were knotted so the knuckles stood white.

"Carl," she exclaimed, "Carl, *min käre*, v'at is wrong?"

"We're assuming," he said as if strangled, "that the human race ought to be continued."

She stood mute. When he turned around again, his features were drawn into rigid lines and he regarded her as if she were an enemy. His tone stayed low, but shaken: "I asked you here for a talk . . . because of something you said yesterday. I see now I played a lousy trick on you. You better go back."

She took a step from him. Courage came. She stiffened her spine. "The first thing you must come to understand, you men," she said with a bite in it, "is that a voman is not a doll. Or a child. I can stand as much as you."

He stared at his boots. "I suppose so," he muttered. "Considering what you've already stood. But for three years, now, I've lived alone with something. Most times I could pretend it wasn't there. But sometimes, lying awake at night—Why should I wish it on to anyone else?"

Her eyes overflowed. She went to him and put her arms about his neck and drew his head down on her shoulder. "Carl, you big brave clever fool, stop trying to carry the universe. I vant to help. That's v'at I am for, you silly!"

After a while he released her and fumbled for his pipe. "Thanks," he said. "Thanks more than I can tell."

She attempted a smile. "Th-th-the best thanks you can give is to be honest vith me. I'm curious, you know."

"Well—" He filled the pipe, ignited the tobacco surrogate and fumed forth clouds. Hands jammed in pockets, he started towards the house. "After all, the item you mentioned gave me hope my nightmare might in fact be wrong. Maybe you won't end up sharing a burden with me. You might lift it off altogether." He paused. "If not, we'll decide between us what to do. Whether to tell the others, ever, or let the knowledge die with us."

She accompanied him inside. A long, airy room, panelled in light wood, carelessly jammed with odd souvenirs and male impedimenta, served him for a private office. She noticed the bunk in one corner and felt the blood mount in head and breast. Then the lustrous blue form of a Monwaingi arose and fluted politely at her. She didn't know whether to be grateful or to swear.

"Miss Holmen, meet Ramri of Tantha," Donnan said. "He's been my sidekick since we first left earth, and my right hand and eye since we got back. I figured he'd better sit in on our discussion. He probably knows more about this civilization-cluster than any other single being."

The delicate fingers felt cool within her own. "Welcome," said the avian in excellent English.

"I cannot express what joy your ship's arrival has given me. For the sake of my friends, and your race, the entire cosmos."

"Takkar så mycket," she whispered, too moved to use any but her father's language.

Donnan gave her a chair and sat down behind the desk. Ramri went back to his sitting-frame. The man puffed hard for a moment before he said roughly:

"The question we have to answer somewhere along the line, or we'll never know where we stand or what to expect, is this. Who destroyed Earth?"

"V'y . . . Kandemir," Sigrid replied, startled. "Is there any doubt?"

"Kandemir has denied it repeatedly. We've ransacked captured archives and interrogated prisoners for a good two years now, ever since Brandobar, without finding any conclusive proof against them. Well, naturally, you say, that don't signify. Knowing how such an act would inflame public opinion against them, they'd take elaborate security precautions. Probably keep no written records whatsoever about the operation, and use hand-picked personnel who'd remain silent unto death. You know how strong clan loyalty is in their upper-echelon families. So Kandemir might or might not be guilty, as far as that goes."

"But the Solar System vas guarded by their missiles!" she protested.

"Yeah," Donnan said. "And isn't that a hell of a clumsy way to preserve the secret? Especially when those missiles were so programmed as to be less than maximum efficient. This is not mere guesswork, based on the chance that the *Europa* and the *Franklin* both managed to escape. Three months ago, I sent an expedition to the Solar System equipped with our new protective gizmos. Arn Goldspring was in charge, and what he can't make a piece of apparatus do isn't worth the trouble. His gang disarmed and captured several missiles, and dissected them down to the last setscrew. They were standard Kandemirian jobs. No doubt about that. But every one had been clumsily programmed. Doesn't that suggest somebody was framing Kandemir?"

"Framing?" Sigrid blinked. "V'at . . . oh, yes. I see. Somevun vanted to make Kandemir seem guilty." She frowned. "Yes, possible. Though v'at ve found v'en ve boarded that vun missile suggests—" She ran out of words.

"That's what I wanted to talk about," said Donnan. "What you found, by a lucky chance, was unique. No such clue turned up in any that Goldspring examined. Did you bring your notes along as I asked?"

She handed them to him. He stared at them while silence stretched. Ramri walked around and looked over his shoulder.

"What d'you make of this?" Donnan asked at length.

"One set of symbols are Kandermirian numerals, of course," Ramri said. "The other . . . I do not know. I may or may not have seen them before. They look almost as if once, long ago, I did. But even in a single cluster, there are so many languages, so many alphabets—" His musings trailed off. Very lightly, he stroked a hand across Donnan's forehead. "Do not let this fret you, Carl-my-friend," he murmured. "Over and over I have told you, what you learned on Katkinu is not the end of all faith. A mistake only. Anyone, any whole race, let alone a few bewildered members of a race, anyone can err. When will you listen to me, and forget what you saw?"

Donnan brushed him away and looked hard at Sigrid. "What did you think of this clue, you ladies?" he asked. "You had three years to mull it over."

"Ve did not think much," she admitted. "There vas so much else to consider, everything ve had lost and everything ve must do to regain our hopes. Ve recognized the numerals. Ve thought maybe the other symbols vere letters. You know, in some obsure Kandemirian alphabet, different from the usual Erzhuat. Just as Europe, Russia, Greece, Israel, China used different languages and alphabets, but the same Arabic numerals. Ve guessed probably these vere notes scribbled for his own guidance by some vorkman helping adjust the missile, who vas not too familiar vith the mechanism."

"There are only six distinct unknown symbols," Donnan grunted, "Not much of an alphabet, if you ask me." He frowned again at the paper.

"They might then be numbers," Ramri offered. "The workman may not have been Kandemirian at all. He could have belonged to a subject race. If the Kandemirians used vassals for the job who were never told what their task was, never even knew what planetary system they were in, that would increase secrecy."

"But the missiles themselves, you dolt!" Donnan snarled. "*They* were the giveaway. What use these fancy precautions if anyone who saw a Mark IV Quester barrelling towards him, and got away, could tell the galaxy it was Kandemirian?"

Ramri left the desk, stared at the floor, and said with sorrow, "Well, you force me, Carl. This was explained to you on Katkinu."

Sigrid watched the paper on the desk as if she could almost read something in those scrawls that it was forbidden to read. "Ve didn't think much about this," she said helplessly. "For vun thing, none of us knew much about Kandemir anyvay, not even Captain Poussin. And vith so much else—Our notes lay forgotten in the ship. Until now."

Realization stabbed home. She gasped, summoned her strength and said harshly, "All right. You have fiddled around plenty long. V'at did they show you on Katkinu?"

Donnan met her gaze blindly. "One more question," he said without tone, "Seems I heard . . . yeah, you've got a Yugoslav and an Israeli aboard, haven't you? Either of them know anything about plans to emigrate from Earth? Were either the

Balkan or Arab countries—the Israelis would be bound to have some idea what the Arabs were up to—either alliance building more ships? Recruiting colonists of any sort?"

"No." Sigrid said.

"You positive?"

"Yes. Surely. Remember, I vas concerned in the pan-European project. I saw shipyards myself, read the journals, heard the gossip. Maybe some very small ships vas being made secretly, but something big enough to take many people to another planet, no. Not at the time ve left. And I don't think there vas time aftervards to build much, before the end came."

"No. There wasn't." Donnan shook himself. "Okay," he said quickly, "that's clue number two you've given me. However fine it would be to have more people alive, I admit I was hoping for the answer you gave. How I was hoping!

"You see, on Katkinu I was shown a film made by the Monwaingi intelligence service. An interview with a trader from Xo, who admitted his combine had sold the Balkan and the Arab alliances something that military theorists once labelled a doomsday weapon. The ultimate deterrent." His voice grew saw-edged. "A set of disruption bombs, able to sterilize the planet. Armed to go off automatically in the event of an attack on the countries possessing same. Got the idea? The Monwaingi believe Earth was not murdered. They think Earth committed suicide."

Sigrid sagged in her chair. A dry little sound

came from her, nothing else was possible. Donnan slammed the desk with his fist. "You see?" he almost shouted. "That's what I didn't want to share. Monwaing was willing to keep the secret. Why shouldn't I? Why let my friends wonder too what race of monsters they belong to? Wonder what's the use of keeping alive, then force themselves to go through the motions anyway—you see?"

He checked himself and went on more quietly: "I've tried to investigate further. Couldn't get any positive information one way or the other from Xo, in spite of some very expensive espionage. Well, naturally, they'd burn their own records of such a transaction. If you sold someone a gun and he turned out to be a homicidal maniac, even if you hadn't known he was, you wouldn't want to admit your part. Would you? Who'd ever come to your gunshop again?

"How do you explain those Kandemirian missiles? Well, Monwaing thinks Kandemir did plant those, but only after the deed was done. To stake a claim. The Solar System is strategically located: outflanks the Monwaingi stars. And when Earth has cooled, it'll be colonized with less difficulty than many other places would give. As for why the missiles are so inefficient, they are intended as a warning rather than an absolute death trap."

"Please note that Kandemir has never denied doing this much. Nor affirmed it, to be sure. But they did announce in their arrogant way that, come the proper time, they would exercise right of salvage; and meanwhile they wouldn't be re-

sponsible for accidents to anyone entering the
Solar System."

Donnan rose. His chair clattered to the floor.
He ignored it, strode around to Sigrid, hunkered
down before her and took her hands. "Okay," he
said suddenly gentle. "You know the worst. I
think we three, here and now, have got all the
clues anyone will ever have for certain. Maybe
we can figure out who the enemy is. Or was.
Buck up, kid. We've got to try."

XV

I tell you naught for your comfort,
  Yea, naught for your desire,
Save that the sky grows darker yet
  And the sea rises higher.

—*Chesterton*

AS IF THRUSTING away an attacker, she sprang to her feet. Donnan went over on his rear. "Oh," she exclaimed. "I'm so sorry." She bent to help him rise. He didn't require her assistance but used it anyway. Their faces came close. He saw her lips stir. Suddenly his own quirked upwards.

"We needed some comic relief," he said. His arm slid down to her waist, lingered there a moment; she laid her head on his shoulder as fleetingly they separated, but he continued to feel where they had touched. Not quite steadily, he went back to his desk, took his pipe and rekindled it.

"I think now I can stand any answer we may find," he said low.

Colour came and went beneath her skin. But she spoke crisply: "Let us list the possibilities. Ve have Kandemir and Earth herself as suspects. But who else? Vorlak? I do not vant to slander an ally, but could . . . v'at you call him . . . Draga Hlott for some reason—"

"No," Donnan said. He explained about the treaty with Russia. "Besides," he added, "as the war developed, I got more and more pipelines into the Vorlakka government. Ger Nenna, one of their scholar-administrator class, was particularly helpful. They, the Dragar, aren't any good at double-dealing. Not only had they no reason to attack Earth—contrariwise—but if they ever did, they wouldn't have operated under cover. And if by some chance they had pulled a sneak assault, they wouldn't have been able to maintain the secret. No, I cleared them long ago."

"Similar considerations apply to the lesser space-faring worlds, like Yann and Unya," Ramri said. "They all feared Kandemir. While the Soviet-Vorlakka agreement was not publicized, everyone knew Earth was as natural prey for the nomads as any other planet and, if the war lasted, would inevitably become involved on the allied side to some degree. Even were they able, no one would have eliminated a potential helper."

"I checked them out pretty thoroughly with espionage just the same," Donnan said bluntly.

"They're clean. The only alternatives are Kandemir and suicide."

Sigrid twisted her hands together. "But suicide does not make sense," she objected. "It is not only that I do not vant to believe it. In some ways it vould be more comfortable to."

"Huh?" Both Donnan and Ramri stared.

"*Ja*, v'y not? Then ve vould know Earth's killers are dead and cannot threaten us any more."

Donnan raised his shoulders and spread his hands. "I'd forgotten women are the cold-blooded, practical sex," he mutterd.

"No, but look, Carl. Let us suppose the doomsday veapon vas actually installed. Then v'y did no country try to plant some people off Earth? Even if, let us say, vuns she had this last resort . . . even if Yugoslavia expected no vun vould dare attack her—still, Yugoslavia vould have been in a better bargaining position yet vith people on other planets. For they could say, v'atever happened, a part of them vould survive. And any other government notified about the veapon vould have tried to take out similar insurance. Insurance against accident, if nothing else. Or against . . . oh . . . blackmail, in case Yugoslavia ever got a nihilist dictator like Hitler vas in his day. So there vould have been *some* emigration from Earth. But ve know for sure there vas not. Even if the emigrants left this cluster, spacemen like Monvaingi vould have noticed it and you vould have heard them talk about it."

Donnan yanked his attention from her to her words. They made sense. He'd speculated along some such lines himself, but had been too shaken emotionally to put his ideas in her cool terms, and too busy making war to straighten out those private horrors that inhibited his reasoning about the subject.

"One possibility," he said. "If Kandemir got wind of the doomsday weapon, Kandemir might'a seized the opportunity, since the destruction of Earth would then be like shooting fish in a barrel. Yugoslavia and the rest might never have had time to organize colonization schemes."

The fair head shook. "I think not," she answered. "Maybe they vere angry men governing Earth's nations, but they vere shrewd too. They had to be. Countries, especially little countries, did not last long in this century if they had stupid leaders. The Balkan and Arab politicians vould have foreseen just the chance of attack you mention. Not only Kandemir, but any planet—any pirate fleet, even, if somebody got vun—anybody could blackmail Earth. No? So I do not think they vould have bought a doomsday veapon unless lots of spaceships vere included in the package."

An eerie tingle moved up Donnan's spine. He smote one fist into the other palm, soundlessly, again and again. "By God, yes," he whispered. "You've hit the point that Monwaing and I both missed. The Monwaingi couldn't be expected to know our psychology that well, I reckon, but I should have seen it. The whole concept of the weapon was lunacy. But lunatics are at least logical thinkers."

Sigrid threw back her shoulders. The lilting voice lifted till it filled the room. "Carl, I do not believe there ever vas any such veapon sold. It just does not figure. Most 'specially not in galactic terms. See, yes, there still vere countries that did not like each other. But those old grudges vere becoming less and less important all the time. There vas still some fighting, but the big atomic var never happened, in spite of almost every country having means to fight it. Does that not show the situation vas stable? That there never vould have been a var? At least not the var everybody vas vorrying about.

"Earth was turning outvards. The old issues vere stopping to matter. Vat vas the use of a doomsday veapon? It vould have been a Chinese vall, built against an enemy that no more existed. For the same price, buying spaceships, buying modern education for the young people, a country could have gained ten times the power . . . and achievement . . . and safety. I tell you, the suicide story is not true."

For a moment neither of the others spoke. They couldn't. Ramri's feathers rose. He swelled his throat pouch and expostulated. "But we know! Our intelligence made that Xoan admit—"

"He lied," Sigrid interrupted. "Is your intelligence alvays correct?"

"Why? Why?" Ramri paced, not as a man does, but in great leaps back and forth between the walls. "What could Xo gain from such a lie? No conceivable advantage! Even the individual who finally confessed, he got nothing but clearance for his ship to leave Monwaing. Absurd!"

Donnan gazed long at his friend before he said, "I think you'd better own up, Ramri: your general staff was had. Let's go on from there."

The end of his nightmare had not eased the wire tautness in him. He bent over the sheet of paper on his desk as if it were an oracular wall. The un-human symbols seemed to intertwine like snakes before his eyes. He focused, instead, on the Roman analogues which had been written in parallel columns.

A B C D E F
M N O P Q MR
BA : PM
ABIJ : MOQMP

Transliteration of some Delphic language—No, no, don't be silly. A through L simply stands for the first twelve numbers of the duodecimal Kandemirian system, with L the sign for zero. So—

It was like a knife-stab. For an instant his heart-beat ceased. He felt a sense of falling. The pulse resumed, crazily, with a roaring in his ears.

As if over immense distances, he heard Ramri say, making an effort at calm:

"By elimination, then, Kandemir does seem to be the murderer planet. Possibly they engineered this Xoan matter as a red herring. And yet I have never felt their guilt was very plausible. That is one reason why I was so quick, however unwilling, to suppose Earth had indeed committed suicide."

"Vell," said the girl, "I am not so familiar with local situations, but I understand that Kandemirians are—or vere, before you broke their power—merciless conquerors. Earth vas still another planet to conquer. And then the Russians actively helped Vorlak."

"Yes, but Tarkamat himself denied to Carl—contemptuously—that the Soviet assistance was significant. Which does sound reasonable. What indeed could a few shiploads of small arms and a handful of student officers amount to, on the scale of interstellar war? If necessary, Kandemir could have lodged a protest with the Soviet government, and made it stick by a threat of punitive action. The Russians would have backed down for certain. Because even a mild raid from Kandemir would have left them so brutally beaten that they would be helpless in the face of their Western rivals. In fact, Tarkamat proved very knowledgeable about Terrestrial politics. He remarked to Carl that if and when he decided to overrun Earth, he would have used native allies more than his own troops. *Divide et impera*, you know. Yet for all the strength and information he had, Tarkamat never even bothered to announce that he knew about the Soviet action.

"Why should he lay Earth waste? Its biochemistry was similar to that of Kandemir. Which made the living planet a far more valuable prize than the present lump of rock, which can only be re-seeded with life at great difficulty and expense, over a period of God knows how long. The nomads are ruthless, but not stupid. Their sole conceivable motive for sterilizing Earth would have been as a terrible object-lesson to their enemies. And then they would have boasted of what they did, not denied it."

Donnan forced himself to take the paper in his hand and punch some keys on his desk calculator. He had never done harder work in his life.

"Yes, yes, you speak sensible," Sigrid was agreeing. "Also, as ve have said, if they vere going to interdict the Solar System, they could have done the job better than vith obsolescent missiles badly programmed. For that matter, Mr. Ramri, v'y should they patrol the System at all? They could have taken it over as part of the general settlement after they von the var, as they expected to vin. Until then, just an occasional visit to make sure nobody vas using it against them would have been enough."

The calculator chattered. Donnan's brain felt like a lump of ice.

"Do you imply that Kandemir never even placed those missiles there?" Ramri asked. "But who did?"

Numbers appeared on the calculator dial. The equation balanced.

Donnan turned around. His voice was flat and empty. "I know who."

"What? *Hvad?*" They stepped closer, saw his expression, and grew still.

An immense, emotionless, steadiness descended on the man. He pointed. "These notes scribbled inside that one missile," he said. "What they were should have been obvious all along. The women failed to see it because they had too much else to think about. They dismissed the whole question as unimportant. But I should have realized the moment I looked. You too, Ramri. I suppose we didn't want to realize."

The golden eyes were level upon him. "Yes? What are those symbols, then, Carl?"

"A conversion table. Jotted down by some technician used to thinking in terms of one number system, who had to adjust instruments and controls calibrated in another system.

"The Kandemirians use a twelve-based arithmetic. These other numerals are based on six."

The girl bit her lip and frowned, puzzled why Donnan was so white. Ramri stood as if carved until, slowly, he spread out his two three-fingered hands.

"It checks," Donnan said. "The initial notation alone, giving the numbers from one to six in parallel rows, is a giveaway. But here are the conversions of some other figures, to which I reckon this or that dial had to be set. The squiggle in between, that Sigrid represented by a colon, has to be an equality sign. BA is 25 in Kandemirian; so is PM in the other system. ABIJ and MOQMP both represent 2134. And so on. No doubt about it."

Ramri made a croaking noise. "A subject race," he managed to articulate. "I, I, I think the Lenyar of Druon . . . the nomads conquered them a long time ago . . . they did formerly employ—"

Donnan shook his head. "Nope," he told him. "Won't do. You yourself just listed the reasons for calling Kandemir innocent of this particular crime."

Understanding came upon Sigrid. She edged away from Ramri, lifting her hands to fend him off. "Monvaing?" she breathed.

"Yes," said Donnan.

"No!" Ramri yelled. "I give you my soul in pawn, it is not true!"

"I never said you were party to the deed yourself," Donnan answered. A dim part of him wanted to take Ramri in his arms, as he had done the day they first saw murdered Earth. But his feet seemed nailed to the floor.

His voice proceeded, oddly echoing within his skull: "Once we grant Monwaing did this, the pieces fall into place. The only objections I can see are that Monwaing wouldn't destroy a good market and a potential ally, and in any event would be too decent to do such a thing.

"But Ramri, Monwaing isn't a single civilization. You didn't recognize these numerals here. Nobody on your planet uses them. However, there are Monwaingi planets you've never seen. And some of the civilizations developed by your race are very hardboiled. The biotechnic orientation. If it's okay to manipulate life in any way convenient, then it's okay to destroy life on any scale convenient. Tantha wouldn't do so; but Laothaung, say, might. And the central government is dominated by Laothaung and similarly minded Societies.

"Those cultures aren't traders, either. Earth as a market meant little to them. What did concern them was Earth as a keg of dynamite. Remember, Resident Wandwai admitted we were too poor and backward as yet to be of military help; and he admitted knowing about that provocative treaty between Russia and Vorlak. Laothaung might well have feared that Kandemir would seize the excuse to invade Earth—thereby spreading the war to Monwaing's most vulnerable flank.

"Oh, they didn't hate humans. I'm sure we survivors would have been well treated, had we stayed in their sectors. But neither did they love us. We, like any living creatures, were just phenomena, to be dealt with as suited their own ends. If they destroyed Earth, they could pin the blame on Kandemir by such methods as planting captured Kandemirian missiles in orbit . . . but not making the missiles too damned effective. That was quite a sound calculation, too. Anger against Kandemir helped out the war effort no end.

"To play safe, they prepared a second-line cover story. I don't know whether the Xoan was bribed or forced to tell that whopper about the doomsday weapon. I do know the story was well concocted, with a lot of detail such as only an alien race that has close acquaintance with Earth could have got straight. However, wasn't it a little too pat that Wandwai had a copy of a top-secret film right in his own regional office? That struck me as odd at the time.

"What else might Monwaing gain by blasting Earth? The planet itself, in due course. They figured on winning any war, as belligerents generally do figure. Because of the ecological differences, Monwaing could only colonize Earth if it was sterile first. Your set-up of many different cultures, each wanting at least one world to itself, makes you actually a good deal more imperialistic than Kandemir ever was. You simply aren't so blunt about it.

"Yeh, I've no doubt left in my mind. Monwaing killed our planet. A real slick job. The only thing they overlooked was what a helpless, fugitive shipload of surviving humans might end up doing. You can't blame them for not foreseeing that. I wouldn't have myself."

Donnan stopped talking.

"You have no proof," Ramri keened.

"No court-room proof," Donnan replied. "Now that we know where to search, though, I don't doubt we can find it."

"What . . . do you plan . . . to do, Carl?"

"I don't know," Donnan admitted heavily. "Sit on the lid till the Kandemirian business is finished, I reckon. Meanwhile we can gather evidence and make ready to act."

Å, *nej*," Sigrid cried out. "Not another var so soon!"

Ramri shuddered. And then the beaked head lifted. Sunlight came in a window and blazed along his feathers. He said, with death in his tone. "That will not be necessary. Not for you."

The frozenness began to break in Donnan. He took an uneven step towards the being who had been his friend. "I never thought *you*—" he stammered. "Only the smallest handful of your race—"

Ramri avoided him. "Of course," he said. "The majority of us shall restore our honour. But this may not be done easily. More than a few individuals must suffer. More, even, than one or two Societies. You need not concern yourselves in this affair, humans. You must not. It is ours.

"I hope the settlement and cleansing need annihilate no more than our mother planet."

He strode jerkily towards the door. "I shall organize the search for positive evidence myself," he said, like a machine, never looking back at them. "When the case is prepared, it shall be put before the proper representatives of each Society. Then the groundwork of action must be quietly laid. I expect our civil war will begin in about one year."

"Ramri, no! Why, your people are the leaders of this whole cluster—"

"You must succeed us."

The Monwaingi went out. Donnan realized he had never known him.

Sigrid came to give the man what comfort she was able. Presently they heard an air-car take off. It hit the sky so fast that it trailed a continuous thunderbolt, as if new armadas were already bound for battle.

They looked at each other. "What have we done?"

ISBN #	Title # Author	Publ. List Price
55979-6	**ACT OF GOD**, Kotani and Roberts	2.95
55945-1	**ACTIVE MEASURES**, David Drake & Janet Morris	3.95
55970-2	**THE ADOLESCENCE OF P-1**, Thomas J. Ryan	2.95
55998-2	**AFTER THE FLAMES**, Silverberg & Spinrad	2.95
55967-2	**AFTER WAR**, Janet Morris	2.95
55934-6	**ALIEN STARS**, C.J. Cherryh, Joe Haldeman & Timothy Zahn, edited by Elizabeth Mitchell	2.95
55978-8	**AT ANY PRICE**, David Drake	3.50
65565-5	**THE BABYLON GATE**, Edward A. Byers	2.95
65586-8	**THE BEST OF ROBERT SILVERBERG**, Robert Silverberg	2.95
55977-X	**BETWEEN THE STROKES OF NIGHT**, Charles Sheffield	3.50
55984-2	**BEYOND THE VEIL**, Janet Morris	15.95
65544-2	**BEYOND WIZARDWALL**, Janet Morris	15.95
55973-7	**BORROWED TIME**, Alan Hruska	2.95
65563-9	**A CHOICE OF DESTINIES**, Melissa Scott	2.95
55960-5	**COBRA**, Timothy Zahn	2.95
65551-5	**COBRA STRIKE!**, Timothy Zahn	3.50
65578-7	**A COMING OF AGE**, Timothy Zahn	3.50
55969-9	**THE CONTINENT OF LIES**, James Morrow	2.95
55917-6	**CUGEL'S SAGA**, Jack Vance	3.50
65552-3	**DEATHWISH WORLD**, Reynolds and Ing	3.50
55995-8	**THE DEVIL'S GAME**, Poul Anderson	2.95
55974-5	**DIASPORAH**, W. R. Yates	2.95
65581-7	**DINOSAUR BEACH**, Keith Laumer	2.95
65579-5	**THE DOOMSDAY EFFECT**, Thomas Wren	2.95
65557-4	**THE DREAM PALACE**, Brynne Stephens	2.95
65564-7	**THE DYING EARTH**, Jack Vance	2.95
55988-5	**FANGLITH**, John Dalmas	2.95
55947-8	**THE FALL OF WINTER**, Jack C. Haldeman II	2.95
55975-3	**FAR FRONTIERS, Volume III**	2.95
65548-5	**FAR FRONTIERS, Volume IV**	2.95
65572-8	**FAR FRONTIERS, Volume V**	2.95
55900-1	**FIRE TIME**, Poul Anderson	2.95
65567-1	**THE FIRST FAMILY**, Patrick Tilley	3.50
55952-4	**FIVE-TWELFTHS OF HEAVEN**, Melissa Scott	2.95
55937-0	**FLIGHT OF THE DRAGONFLY**, Robert L. Forward	3.50
55986-9	**THE FORTY-MINUTE WAR**, Janet Morris	3.50
55971-0	**FORWARD**, Gordon R. Dickson	2.95
65550-7	**THE FRANKENSTEIN PAPERS**, Fred Saberhagen	3.50
55899-4	**FRONTERA**, Lewis Shiner	2.95
55918-4	**THE GAME BEYOND**, Melissa Scott	2.95
55959-1	**THE GAME OF EMPIRE**, Poul Anderson	3.50
65561-2	**THE GATES OF HELL**, Janet Morris	14.95
65566-3	**GLADIATOR-AT-LAW**, Pohl and Kornbluth	2.95
55904-4	**THE GOLDEN PEOPLE**, Fred Saberhagen	3.50
65555-8	**HEROES IN HELL**, Janet Morris	3.50
65571-X	**HIGH JUSTICE**, Jerry Pournelle	2.95

ISBN #	Title # Author	Publ. List Price
55930-3	HOTHOUSE, Brian Aldiss	2.95
55905-2	HOUR OF THE HORDE, Gordon R. Dickson	2.95
65547-7	THE IDENTITY MATRIX, Jack Chalker	2.95
65569-8	I, MARTHA ADAMS, Pauline Glen Winslow	3.95
55994-X	INVADERS, Gordon R. Dickson	2.95
55993-1	IN THE FACE OF MY ENEMY, Joe Delaney	2.95
65570-1	JOE MAUSER, MERCENARY, Reynolds and Banks	2.95
55931-1	KILLER, David Drake & Karl Edward Wagner	2.95
55996-6	KILLER STATION, Martin Caidin	3.50
65559-0	THE LAST DREAM, Gordon R. Dickson	2.95
55981-8	THE LIFESHIP, Dickson and Harrison	2.95
55980-X	THE LONG FORGETTING, Edward A. Byers	2.95
55992-3	THE LONG MYND, Edward Hughes	2.95
55997-4	MASTER OF SPACE AND TIME, Rudy Rucker	2.95
65573-6	MEDUSA, Janet and Chris Morris	3.50
65562-0	THE MESSIAH STONE, Martin Caidin	3.95
55580-9	MINDSPAN, Gordon R. Dickson	2.95
65553-1	THE ODYSSEUS SOLUTION, Banks and Lambe	2.95
55926-5	THE OTHER TIME, Mack Reynolds with Dean Ing	2.95
55965-6	THE PEACE WAR, Vernor Vinge	3.50
55982-6	PLAGUE OF DEMONS, Keith Laumer	2.75
55966-4	A PRINCESS OF CHAMELN, Cherry Wilder	2.95
65568-X	RANKS OF BRONZE, David Drake	3.50
65577-9	REBELS IN HELL, Janet Morris, et. al.	3.50
55990-7	RETIEF OF THE CDT, Keith Laumer	2.95
65556-6	RETIEF AND THE PANGALACTIC PAGEANT OF PULCHRITUDE, Keith Laumer	2.95
65575-2	RETIEF AND THE WARLORDS, Keith Laumer	2.95
55902-8	THE RETURN OF RETIEF, Keith Laumer	2.95
55991-5	RHIALTO THE MARVELLOUS, Jack Vance	3.50
65545-0	ROGUE BOLO, Keith Laumer	2.95
65554-X	SANDKINGS, George R.R. Martin	2.95
65546-9	SATURNALIA, Grant Callin	2.95
55989-3	SEARCH THE SKY, Pohl and Kornbluth	2.95
55914-1	SEVEN CONQUESTS, Poul Anderson	2.95
65574-4	SHARDS OF HONOR, Lois McMaster Bujold	2.95
55951-6	THE SHATTERED WORLD, Michael Reaves	3.50
	THE SILISTRA SERIES	
55915-X	RETURNING CREATION, Janet Morris	2.95
55919-2	THE GOLDEN SWORD, Janet Morris	2.95
55932-X	WIND FROM THE ABYSS, Janet Morris	2.95
55936-2	THE CARNELIAN THRONE, Janet Morris	2.95
65549-3	THE SINFUL ONES, Fritz Leiber	2.95
65558-2	THE STARCHILD TRILOGY, Pohl and Williamson	3.95
55999-0	STARSWARM, Brian Aldiss	2.95
55927-3	SURVIVAL!, Gordon R. Dickson	2.75
55938-9	THE TORCH OF HONOR, Roger Macbride Allen	2.95

ISBN #	Title # Author	Publ. List Price
55942-7	TROJAN ORBIT, Mack Reynolds with Dean Ing	2.95
55985-0	TUF VOYAGING, George R.R. Martin	15.95
55916-8	VALENTINA, Joseph H. Delaney & Marc Steigler	3.50
55898-6	WEB OF DARKENSS, Marion Zimmer Bradley	3.50
55925-7	WITH MERCY TOWARD NONE, Glen Cook	2.95
65576-0	WOLFBANE, Pohl and Kornbluth	2.95
55962-1	WOLFLING, Gordon R. Dickson	2.95
55987-7	YORATH THE WOLF, Cherry Wilder	2.95
55906-0	THE ZANZIBAR CAT, Joanna Russ	3.50

COMPUTER BOOKS AND GENERAL INTEREST NONFICTION

ISBN #	Title # Author	Publ. List Price
55968-0	ADVENTURES IN MICROLAND, Jerry Pournelle	9.95
55933-8	AI: HOW MACHINES THINK, F. David Peat	8.95
55922-2	THE ESSENTIAL USER'S GUIDE TO THE IBM PC, XT, AND PCjr., Dian Girard	6.95
55940-0	EUREKA FOR THE IBM PC AND PCjr, Tim Knight	7.95
55941-9	THE FUTURE OF FLIGHT, Leik Myrabo with Dean Ing	7.95
55955-9	THE GUIDEBOOK FOR WINNING ADVENTURERS, David & Sandy Small	8.95
55923-0	MUTUAL ASSURED SURVIVAL, Jerry Pournelle and Dean Ing	6.95
55929-X	PROGRAMMING LANGUAGES: FEATURING THE IBM PC, Marc Stiegler & Bob Hansen	9.95
55963-X	THE SERIOUS ASSEMBLER, Charles Crayne & Dian Girard Crayne	8.95
55907-9	THE SMALL BUSINESS COMPUTER TODAY AND TOMORROW, William E. Grieb, Jr.	6.95
55921-4	THE USER'S GUIDE TO CP/M SYSTEMS, Tony Bove & Cheryl Rhodes	8.95
55948-6	THE USER'S GUIDE TO FREE SOFTWARE, Tony Bove & Cheryl Rhodes	9.95
55908-7	THE USER'S GUIDE TO SMALL COMPUTERS, Jerry Pournelle	9.95

Here is an excerpt from the newest novel by Martin Caidin, to be published in September 1986 by Baen Books:

MARTIN CAIDIN
ZOBOA

The senior officer on duty on the flight line of Guantanamo Air Base on the southern coastline of Cuba checked the time, made a notation on his clipboard, and lifted his head as a buzzer affixed to his ear rattled his skull. He turned. They were right on time. Captain Jeff Baumbach moved his hand more by reflex than directed thought to check the .357 Magnum on his hip. He gestured at the armored vehicle slowing at the gate, its every movement covered by heavy automatic cannon.

"Check 'em *all* out!" Baumbach called. Military Police motioned the truck in between heavy barricades until it was secured. They checked the identity passes of every man, went through, atop and beneath the vehicle, finally sent it through the final barricade to the flight line where two machine gun-armed jeeps rolled alongside as escort. The armored truck stopped by an old Convair 440 twin-engined transport with bright lettering on each side of its fuselage. The cargo doors of the transport of ST. THOMAS ORCHARD FARMS opened wide. The crew wore Air Force fatigues and all carried sidearms.

A master sergeant studied the truck and the men. "Move it, move it," he said impatiently. "Load 'em up. We're behind schedule."

Four cases moved with exquisite care from the truck to the loading conveyor to the aircraft. Each case carried the same identifying line but differing serial numbers. It didn't really matter. NUCLEAR WEAPON MARK 62 is enough of a grabber without any silly serial number.

The bombs were loaded and secured with steel cabling and heavy webbing tiedowns, men signed their names and exchanged papers, doors slammed closed, and the right engine of the Convair whined as the pilots brought power to the metal bird. . . .

In central Florida, horses moved through the tall morning-wet grass of a remote field. It is an ordinary scene of an ordinary Florida ranch . . . until the trees and the fences begin to move.

Tractors pulled the trees, tugging with steel cables to move the wheeled dollies from the soft ground. Pickup trucks and jeeps latched on to fence ends and moved slowly to swing the fences at enormous hinges. Within minutes a clear path seven thousand feet from north to south had been created, and the whine of machinery sounded over the staccato beating of equine hooves. Men kept the animals clear of field center, where high grass moved as if by magic to reveal an asphalted airstrip beneath. Still invisible to any eye, powerful jet engines rose from a deep-throated whine to ear-twisting shrieks and the cry of acetylene torches. Shouting male voices diminish to feeble cries in the rising crescendo of power, and workers move hastily aside as the front of a hill disappears into the ground and two jet fighters roll forward slowly, bobbing on their nose gear.

"Sir, they're loading now," the controller tells the lead pilot, knowing the second man also listens. "Are you ready to copy? I have their time hack for takeoff and the stages for their route."

The man in the lead jet fighter responds in flawless Arabic. "Quickly; I copy. And do not speak English again." ...

"Orchard One, you're clear to the active and clear for takeoff. Over."

Captain Jim Mattson pressed his yoke transmit button. "Ah, roger Gitmo Control. Orchard One clear for the active and rolling takeoff. Over."

"Orchard One, it's all yours. Over."

"Roger that, Gitmo. Orchard One is rolling." Mattson advanced the throttles steadily, his copilot, John Latimer, placing his left hand securely atop the knuckles of his pilot. The convair sped toward the ocean, lifted smoothly and began its long climbing turn over open water. ...

The horses shied nervously with the relentless howl of the jet fighter engines. Everyone on the field waited for the right words to pass between the controller in his underground bunker on the side of the runway and the two men in the fighter cockpits. A headset in the lead fighter hummed.

"Control here."

"Go ahead."

"Your quarry is in the air. Confirm ready."

The pilots glanced at one another. "Allah One ready."

"Allah Two waits."

"Very good, sirs. Three minutes, sirs." ...

They came out of the sun, silvery streaks trailing the unsuspecting shape of Orchard One. Their presence remained unknown until the instant a powerful electronic jammer in the rear cockpit of the lead T-33 broadcast its signal to overpower any electronics aboard the Convair. The shriek pierced the eardrums of the Convair's radioman and he ripped off his headset. In the cockpit, Captain John Latimer, flying right seat, mirrored the reaction to the icepick scream in their ears. Instinct brought Captain Jim Mattson's hands to the yoke. But the automatic pilot held true, and the Convair did not wave or tremble. Only the radio and electronics systems had seemingly gone mad. The flight engineer rushed to the cockpit, squeezed Mattson's shoulder, and shouted to him. "Sir! To our left! There!"

They looked out to see the all-black fighter with Arabic lettering on the fuselage and tail. The pilot's face was concealed behind an oxygen mask and goldfilm visor. "Who the hell is that?" Mattson wondered aloud, and in the same breath turned to Latimer. "You all right?"

Latimer sat back, shaking his head to clear the battering echoes in his brain. He nodded. "Yeah, sure; fine. What the hell was that?"

The radioman wailed painfully into the flight deck with them, his face furrowed in pain. "Jamming . . . somehow they're jamming us. They must have, God, I don't know . . . but I can't get out on anything."

They exchanged glances. Not a single word was needed to confirm that they were in deep shit. Nobody shows up in a black T-33 jet fighter with Arabic markings and knocks out all radio frequencies unless they're a nasty crowd with killing on their minds. Mattson instantly became the professional military pilot.

"Emergency beacon?"

"No joy, sir. Blocked."

"Anybody see more than one fighter out—"

The answer came in a hammering vibration that blurred their sight. The Convair yawed sharply to the right as metal exploded far out on the right wing. "There's another one out there, all right!" Latimer shouted. "He just shot the hell out of the wing! He's coming alongside—"

They watched the black fighter slide into perfect formation to their right and just above their mangled wingtip. His dive brake extended. The pilot pointed down with his forefinger and then his landing gear extended.

"Jesus Christ!" Latimer exclaimed. "He's ordered us to land!"

"Screw that," Mattson snarled. "Sparks! Get Patrick Control and tell them we're under attack. We need—"

"Sir, goddamnit! I can't get out on any frequency!"

Glowing tracers lashed the air before the Convair. The T-33 on their left had eased back and above to give them another warning burst. They looked out at the fighter to their right. The pilot tapped his left wrist to signify his watch, then drew a finger across his throat.

SEPTEMBER 1986 • 65588-4 • 448 pp. • $3.50

To order any Baen Book by mail, send the cover price plus 75¢ for first-class postage and handling to: Baen Books, Dept. BA, 260 Fifth Avenue, New York, N.Y. 10001.